Building
Love

By M. E. Tudor

Other Books by M. E. Tudor

Suddenly

Second Chances

The Wrong Place at the Right Time

Judge Not

Treacherous Souls

Afternoon Delight

Taste Testing

Standing Her Ground

The Perfect Proposal

Visit M. E. Tudor's website for more information

www.metudor.com

This book is dedicated to my seven grandchildren, four of which I had the honor of being present when they came into this world. There is nothing more amazing to experience than the birth of a child.

Chapter One
Patty

"Have you lost your mind?" That was all I could think to say when Mom took me to see the house she had just bought. It looked like the left behind set of an awful horror movie.

"No, Patricia, I have not lost my mind," Mom said indignantly. She walked into what I assumed had been the living room and turned in a circle. "It just needs some tender loving care and elbow grease."

I raised both eyebrows and looked down at my protruding stomach. "Well, I hope you realize that it will be at least two months before I will be lending much elbow grease."

Mom came over and put her arm around my shoulders. "Yes, I know there will be a limit to what you can help with, but there is still a lot you can do. You can sweep stuff into a pile, and I'll pick it up." She grabbed a piece of the peeling wallpaper and pulled it off the wall. "You can help strip the wallpaper."

I'm not afraid of hard work. There were many weekends, summers, and school breaks that I'd spent working alongside my parents on one job site or another. My father had been a painter and drywall finisher by trade. My mother had worked with him for as long as I could remember, so she was capable of doing a lot of the drywall finishing and painting that this place was going to need. I looked around the room. This project was going to take a lot more than stripping wallpaper and patching the walls to make it livable.

"Are you sure it's safe to walk around in here?" I asked looking at the scuffed wood floors.

"Yes," Mom said. "I had a building inspector go over every nook and cranny. He said the house was structurally sound. It just needs some cosmetic work.

I looked at her. "Cosmetic work? I think a wrecking crew might be more useful."

She scowled at me. "It's not that bad." She looked up at the place where a light fixture had been hanging that was just loose wires now. "Anyway, I've got a contractor friend who's going to take a look at it for me. He promised to give me a good deal based on us doing a lot of the work."

Shaking my head, I followed behind Mom as she took me on a tour of the whole house. I listened as she told me about her plans for each room.

Mom had been talking about owning a bed and breakfast for many years. It was something Dad and she had planned to do together. When he was killed by a drunk driver a little over a year ago, all of Mom's dreams seemed to disappear.

This year had been really hard on both of us. We lost the home Mom and Dad had just purchased less than six months before his accident because his life insurance company and the drunk driver's car insurance company were stalling on giving Mom the money she was due. Mom hired an excellent lawyer who finally got her all the money she was supposed to get and a little more for pain and suffering. The money had just come in, and that was how Mom had bought this monstrosity.

We have been living in a tiny two-bedroom low-income apartment while we waited for the settlement. Now that the money had finally come in, we had just a few weeks to get a new place.

When Mom told me she was going to look at a house or two the other day, I never expected her to buy something so quickly. However, when she told me what she paid for this place, I wasn't surprised she'd jumped on the opportunity. It was cheap, but now I know why.

After we'd finished the tour of the upstairs, we returned to the living room. "So what do you think?" Mom asked.

Slipping my arm around her narrow waist, I looked around the room again. I couldn't see the potential, but apparently, Mom could. If she wanted to turn this house into a bed and breakfast, I would help her as much as possible. "When you said you bought a house to turn into a bed and breakfast, I pictured something a little more ready to be moved into."

Mom grinned. "I'm sure you did, but I couldn't pass up this deal. The great-grandson of the original owner was selling the property because he was tired of dealing with it. I offered him a bid, and he took it." She turned to me. "I know I probably should have talked to you about it before I bought it because some of that money is yours. But, once we get this up and running, you won't have to worry about getting a babysitter for Mattie because you can help me run the bed and breakfast. Do you think you would want to do that?"

She had a point about the babysitter. I have been worried about having to get a job and leaving the baby with a stranger. This way I could be home with Mattie. "Yes, I want to do that. When do we start?"

Mom leaned over, kissed me on my cheek, and patted my enormous belly. "This weekend."

I rubbed the spot Mom had patted and felt the tiny foot of the little girl I was carrying kick my hand. When I first found out I was pregnant, I had been completely devastated. Having a baby this early in my life had not been part of my plans, but now I couldn't wait for her to get here. Partially because I'm sick of feeling like a beached whale, but mostly because I couldn't wait to hold my little girl in my arms.

"Okay," I said and followed Mom outside.

"What does Mattie feel like having for dinner?" Mom asked.

I ran my hands over my stomach and leaned down as if to talk to the baby. "What do you think Matilda, Chinese, or Italian? One kick for Chinese. Two for Italian." The baby's answer was a single solid kick to my ribs.

I rubbed the spot where she'd planted her foot and said, "Chinese it is."

Mom leaned down and kissed my belly. "Good choice, Mattie. That's what Grandma wanted too."

I shook my head. My mother is a fantastic person. We had been a close family unit before my dad died. After he died, I lost my mind for a little while and started being an idiot out partying and trying to bury my pain in drugs and alcohol. I had been terrified to tell Mom about my pregnancy after I first found out. She had just lost her husband, and then her only daughter became an out of control punk worrying her to death.

Mom had not been as upset as I thought she would be. Granted, she had not been happy with me, but I wasn't thrilled with me either. Selfish is the kindest word I can think of to describe myself for those first six months after Dad died. I was so wrapped up in my own pain that I had not considered how hard things were for Mom. It took me becoming pregnant and realizing the depth of that responsibility before I could see what I was doing to her. Now, I'm determined to make up for my bad choices by helping Mom as much as I can.

I looked around the overgrown yard as we closed the front door. This house was going to be a massive project. I wonder if Mom really understood how much work it was going to take to make this place livable, let alone ready for paying guests. It didn't matter. If Mom thinks it can be done, then I'm going to do whatever it takes to help make it happen.

Chapter Two
Theresa

I looked up from the pictures I was studying when my father walked into the office we share.

"What's new?" he asked.

"Just looking at the pictures of Mrs. Doan's yard," I said. "She wants a path to the pergola made with stepping stones, and she gave me a list of the new flowers and bushes she'd like to have, so I'm trying to figure out how to best organize the flower beds."

He nodded and moved to look over my shoulder at the pictures. "About how long do you think that will take?"

"A week, maybe a week and a half," I answered. "The hardest part is going to be digging the new gardens, but John and Jesus will make quick work of it. Why?"

"I might have a remodel job for you," Dad said. "It's going to be a pretty big job and will probably take at least a couple months. You interested?"

"You sure you trust me with that big a job?" I asked, surprised.

Dad shrugged and walked away, going to his desk and sitting down in his oversized leather chair. "It's for an old friend. She's on a tight budget. I figure you can do it for less than I can. There will be a lot of work you can do yourself and not bring a crew in, so more of the money will go in your pocket. Plus there are some things she wants to do herself to save money, and it will let me see how you do with a project like this. Not all my clients can afford to pay top dollar for a big and fast crew to come through and be done in a couple of weeks."

"Okay, sure, I'd love to take on a remodel. What's it entail?"

"Before you say yes for certain, how about we go out to the house this afternoon so you can see what you're getting into," Dad suggested.

I nodded. "Okay."

A couple of hours later, Dad and I got in his maroon crew cab diesel truck and headed toward the downtown area. Riverton is a small city that has become known for its arts and crafts festivals. The downtown area is in the process of being rejuvenated. Lots of little shops have opened since the city has started promoting tourism in the town's historic district.

Many people were buying the old, dilapidated homes and making them into beautiful showpieces while still keeping their historical value. That's why I wasn't surprised that the house I was going to be working on was in the historic district.

We turned onto Fourth Street, and Dad stopped in front of a two-story brick house in pressing need of repair.

"Is this it?" I asked, getting out of the truck.

"Yep. My friend, Mandy wants to turn it into a bed and breakfast," Dad said as he came around the truck and stood beside me.

Crossing my arms over my chest, I looked at the overgrown yard and rundown house. "This is going to take a lot of work."

"Yeah? Wait until you see the inside," Dad said and took a key out of his pocket. "Come on, let's have a look."

I followed him up the broken sidewalk to the front door. The inside of the house had a strong musk scent from years of being closed up. The wallpaper was peeling off the walls showing the old and cracking drywall underneath. Spider webs were everywhere. I hate spiders.

"Is this place livable?" I asked as I walked across the hardwood floor leading into a large room with a fireplace.

"Mandy had a building inspector to come out and look at it before she bought it. The structure is sound," Dad said, looking around. "It's just going to need a lot of work."

"Yeah," I agreed.

We walked through the downstairs rooms. The kitchen looked like its last renovation was in the 1950s. There was one bathroom downstairs, and all that was left in there were the pipes. The floor looked like it might need replacing too.

I followed Dad upstairs where there were four more rooms, all of which had most likely been bedrooms.

"No bathroom up here?" I asked.

"No," Dad said. "The house was built in the early 1900s and had been used as a single family rental since the 80s. It has sat empty for the most of the last five years. The guy who sold it to Mandy was the great-grandson of the original owner. I don't think he's done anything to it since he inherited it. His father had at least sent someone to mow and keep an eye on the house. I think the great-grandson decided to get rid of it rather than fix it up."

"Wow," I said. "So what kind of budget are we talking about?"

"Maybe fifty thousand," he said.

I looked at him incredulously. "You expect me to turn this into a bed and breakfast for under fifty thousand dollars?"

"It's doable," Dad said. "And I have faith that you can pull it off. Mandy and her daughter will do some of the work, cleaning the place up and stuff like that, so that will cut down on what you have to pay out for labor."

I stood looking around the room with my hands on my hips. I wasn't sure I could do it for that little money, but when Dad asked me if I accepted the challenge, I said, "Yes."

The owner and I would definitely have to go over what she wanted explicitly. This house was not going to be an easy project to keep within the budget, but I would sure try.

Chapter Three
Patty

I was craving sushi, which I had never tried until I became pregnant. Both my parents loved sushi, but I'd always turned my nose up at the thought of eating raw fish. Mom and I had been in this very restaurant not long after I found out I was pregnant. She had a sushi sampler platter and something about the way it smelled made my mouth water. Mom had been stunned when I'd picked up a piece of nigiri sushi and popped it in my mouth. I was hooked after that.

Mom was already at our table by the time I'd filled my plate with everything I was craving. She looked at my plate filled with mostly seafood and said, "Mattie's going to come out part fish."

I laughed. "What's wrong with that?"

"Nothing, then it won't take as long for her to like sushi as it did you," Mom said and swiped a shrimp tempura roll off my plate.

We were about halfway through our dinner when I saw Mom look past my shoulder and smile. I turned to see who had made her light up like that as a tall, handsome man approached our table with a girl I recognized from school. She was a few years older than me and had graduated already, but I remembered that she had been a basketball player for the girls' team and part of the art and theatre group. It was the same clique I had ended up joining my junior year.

"Hi, Richard," Mom said enthusiastically and stood to hug the man.

They both turned to me, and he said, "My goodness, Patty. You have grown into quite a beautiful young lady."

I wiped my mouth with my napkin to cover my blush. "Thank you. I don't think I know you though," I said.

"You probably don't remember me," Richard said. "You were what..." he turned to look at Mom for confirmation, "six or seven the last time I saw you?"

"That's probably right," Mom agreed. She reached her hand out to the girl and said, "And you must be Theresa? I'm Mandy McNeal."

"Yes," Theresa said in a deep, but quiet voice as she took Mom's hand.

"You definitely wouldn't remember me. You were just a baby the last time I saw you," Mom said.

"So how do you two know each other," I asked, noting the shy looks Richard and Mom were giving each other.

"We went to high school together," Mom said. "We were close friends."

Richard nodded and smiled at Mom causing her to blush deeply. "Yes, we were friends."

Out of the corner of my eye, I saw Theresa roll her eyes much the same way I wanted to. Clearly, they had been more than friends.

"Do you guys want to join us?" Mom asked Richard, and then looked at me. "You wouldn't mind, would you, Patty?"

Before I could answer, Richard said, "How about we sit here at the table next to you? That way we won't be too crowded in that small booth."

"That's a good idea," Mom said.

I was relieved because the booth we were in was rather small. I was already taking up the most of my side with my large stomach.

A waitress came around and asked them what they wanted to drink. Richard ordered sake and a Chinese beer. Theresa asked for hot tea.

When Richard and Theresa left to go to the buffet, I pinned Mom with a questioning look. "What?" she asked and stuffed some rice into her mouth.

"Just friends? Really?" I asked.

Mom blushed crimson. "It was a long time ago, before your father."

I smiled and picked up a California roll with my chopsticks. "And you've recently run into each other? Mom, this town is not that big."

Mom looked over her shoulder and saw that Richard was coming back. "We'll talk about it later."

"Yes, we will," I agreed.

Richard surprised me by sitting at his table next to me. I would have thought he would want to sit closer to Mom, but I quickly figured out that this way he could look straight at her while they talked rather than having to look sideways at her. Smart man. But, that also put Theresa facing my direction. She smiled at me, almost apologetically, when she first sat down with her plate that looked similar to the way mine had when I'd first come back from the buffet. Theresa apparently liked seafood too.

"I was telling Theresa about your project earlier," Richard said. "I'm going to give the job to her if you don't care."

Mom looked a little surprised and disappointed. "I thought you'd be working on it."

"I'll be out there to check on the progress for sure," Richard assured her. "But, Theresa is very good with remodeling jobs. In fact, it's her specialty. She worked for me while she was in high school and going to the technical college. Since she finished school, I've been giving her more and more of my remodeling contracts to oversee." He looked at Theresa and then smiled at my mom. "She has built a very nice portfolio in the past two years that you can take a look at to see what she has already done."

"Yours will be the biggest job I've done so far, but I've done several smaller jobs that entailed pretty much everything we will be doing overall with your project," Theresa assured her.

Mom still looked a bit concerned, but said, "I'll take a look at her portfolio, and we'll go from there."

"Great," Richard said, seeming confident that Mom would agree to let his daughter run the remodel job of her bed and breakfast. He turned to me and changed the subject. "Your mom tells me you are quite the artist. What medium do you like to work with?"

His question took me by surprise. Only people familiar with art would ask you what medium you prefer. "Charcoal is what I work with most, but I'm also partial to pastels."

"Oil or chalk?" he asked before putting a sushi roll in his mouth.

"Both," I said.

He nodded in Theresa's direction. "Theresa has always used pencils and tempera paint."

"I don't have the patience to wait for oil paint to dry," Theresa said, her dark eyes capturing mine.

"Me either," I agreed and turned to Mom, needing releasing from Theresa's intense gaze. It was weird, but her looking so directly into my eyes unnerved me a little.

"Wasn't oil your favorite?" Richard asked Mom.

"Yes. I used to have the patience of a saint," Mom said and looked pointedly at me, "until the teenage years."

Richard laughed. It was a hearty warm sound, and I found myself grinning. "Yes, Theresa and her brother, Jonah, both ruined whatever patience I used to have."

"Mostly Jonah and Mother," Theresa muttered.

Mom looked at Richard. "So Jonah went with Deidre?"

Richard poured some sake in the tiny cup and sipped from it. "Yeah, he always was a bit of a momma's boy." That elicited an eye roll from Theresa. "Plus, he would never work with me as Theresa has. He always hated to get dirty."

Theresa rolled her eyes again. "He doesn't want to work, period." Her father gave her a warning glare. "What?" she asked before deliberately taking a large bite of an egg roll.

I couldn't help but grin. I knew Jonah. He had been in the grade above me. Theresa was right; he was one of those people who expected to be given everything. I'd always assumed it was because his parents had money. Garland Construction was one of the largest construction companies in western Kentucky. I was actually surprised by how down to earth Richard Garland seemed to be compared to his son.

Theresa had been a junior when I was a freshman. She had run some with the popular crowd and some with the art geeks. I'd seen her a few times in the halls, but we'd never said more than a handful of words to each other. I have no idea what she was like back then, but she seemed very mature now.

After draining his sake cup and chasing it with beer, Richard said, "That was his mother's doing."

Theresa looked at Mom and grinned. "It was because I refused to be a princess. I liked getting messy, still do."

Mom smiled. "Ah, so since she couldn't mold you into her perfect little girl, she decided to make your brother into the perfect little boy?"

"Something like that," Richard said and changed the subject again. "So where are you working now, Mandy? I know you'd worked with Pat a lot before…" His comment trailed off, and he gave Mom a sad look. Clearing his throat, he asked, "Do you still paint as a sub-contractor?"

"No," Mom said sadly. "I still haven't been able to do more than put Pat's tools in storage. I've been working at Simpson Concrete as a secretary. It's simple work and pays okay."

Richard nodded and sipped his beer. "So, let's talk about what you want to do to that house."

The rest of the meal was spent talking about how Mom wanted to have our living quarters downstairs and make three of the rooms upstairs guest rooms and one into a bathroom.

Theresa had pulled a sketch pad out of a bag that I had not noticed she had been carrying. She leafed past several sketches of plants and animals before finding a blank page. I was impressed by how quickly she could sketch each room and give them life in the way Mom wanted them to look. By the time we had finished our meals, I was pretty sure that Theresa had convinced Mom that she was perfectly capable of doing the remodel of the house.

As we all walked out to our cars, Mom turned to Theresa and said, "Will you have time later this week to show me your portfolio?

"Sure." She handed Mom a business card and said, "Just give me a call, and we'll set up a time."

I watched Theresa, and her father get into Richard's big truck. There was something about her that was tickling my memory, but I couldn't put my finger on it.

"What do you think?" Mom asked as we got in her car.

I shrugged. "Theresa talked like she knew what she was doing."

"That's what I thought too," Mom agreed.

As I put on my seatbelt, I turned to her and said, "Now, why don't you tell me about you and Richard."

Chapter Four
Theresa

"Did you know her daughter was pregnant?" I asked Dad as we drove home.

"Yes, we talked about it a little the day she came by the office to talk to me about the house," he said.

"Where was I?" I asked.

"You were at Mrs. Doan's house," he answered.

I didn't say anything for a few minutes, but I was dying to know what happened. I hadn't known Patty at school, but I'd watched her from afar. I'd thought she was beautiful the first time I saw her. She had long silky auburn tresses and deep green eyes. Admittedly, I'd developed a little crush on her back then. "So is she getting married to the father?" I asked.

My father glanced over at me and then back on the road. He seemed to be mulling over what he was going to tell me about what he knew, which, of course, made me even more curious. Finally, he said, "The father is a loser bastard who refuses to claim the baby."

Just his tone told me that he knew who the father was and disliked him, a lot.

"Trying to get out of paying child support, no doubt," I said.

"Something like that," Dad muttered.

I decided to leave the topic alone for now since it seemed to have put him in a mood. Changing the subject, I said, "You think Mandy will still go with us knowing that I'm the one running the show?"

"Oh yeah," Dad said, clearly relieved to be off the baby subject. "She knows I'll keep an eye on the project and make sure you do things right." He grinned at me. "Although, I have no doubt you'll do a great job."

"Thanks," I said, appreciating his faith in me.

We were quiet for a few minutes before I finally asked, "So how do you know Mandy?"

I could see him blushing in the darkness. "We dated in high school before I got with your mom."

"How did she know me as a baby?"

Dad sighed. "We had remained friends after we split up. Your mom and I had our ups and downs, and Mandy was a friend with whom I could confide. When your Mom became pregnant with you, she insisted I stop being friends with Mandy."

"You're kidding?" I asked, not all that shocked considering what a bitch my mother is.

"No," Dad said. "It was hard because your mother was horrible to live with when she was pregnant. We were living with my parents in an apartment above the garage. I wasn't sure we were going to make it through her pregnancy, but I hung on, mostly because my mother would not hear of me leaving Deidre. She didn't like her, but Mom came from a strict upbringing, and you did not shirk your responsibilities, especially when it came to fathering a child."

"Were you ever in love with Mom?" We'd never really talked about their relationship because I've always felt it was my fault my parents split up.

Dad sighed. "On and off. She drove me absolutely insane, but then she would turn soft and kind, and I'd fall all over again. After you were born, there was no way I was leaving. Dad made me a foreman, and I was running several jobs, and life was good for a while."

"What happened?"

"Mandy's husband, Pat McNeal got a job working for our company. He and Mandy had just gotten married. Mandy would come out to the jobs sometimes. That's when she would see you. I often took you with me to jobs when I was just checking on things, especially if your mother acted like she was having a meltdown. Pat and I became friends, and Mandy and I picked up like we'd never stopped being friends. Pat talked Mandy into working with him, and the two of them were a fantastic team.

"Your mother was pissed when she found out that Mandy was on the job sites. The next thing I knew she was pregnant with Jonah. She was calling me so much it was a wonder that I got anything done. After Jonah was born, I never had time to do anything but work. I had to come straight home and take care of you because she couldn't handle both of you."

Shaking my head, I said, "And yet young women like Patty raise kids on their own all the time."

"Yep," Dad agreed. "Anyway, Pat and Mandy continued to subcontract for us until he got a contract with Wellington Painters, so I didn't see them much after that. They often brought Patty to the job sites with them, especially on the weekends. Patty was probably six the last time Pat and Mandy worked for us."

"That explains why I didn't remember seeing her before high school. I'm sure I would have remembered seeing her on a job site."

I didn't realize that I had said that out loud until Dad asked, "Did you know her in high school?"

I shook my head. "No, she was a freshman when I was a junior."

"I wonder if she knew Jonah back then," Dad said. "They are just a year apart."

"Probably, the underclassmen would have shared the same halls," I said. "Plus they probably went to junior high together too." All of the elementary schools in the west part of our county sent their kids to the same middle school and high school. I know Patty didn't go to our elementary school because I would have remembered her if she had.

I was thankful when Dad changed the subject and asked, "Whatcha going to do when we get home?"

"Go to bed," I said as a yawn overtook me. "I'm planning to meet John and Jesus at Mrs. Doan's at seven, so we can start making the new gardens."

"That's early isn't it?" Dad asked. "I would think a retired lady like Mrs. Doan would want to sleep in."

"Are you kidding," I said. "She wanted us there at five, but I told her I didn't think her neighbors would appreciate hearing a bunch of people and power tools in her yard that early in the morning."

Dad laughed. "Yeah, that's not a good way to make an impression on potential customers."

The rest of the trip was made in silence. I couldn't get over that Patty McNeal was very pregnant. She had to be at least six months along. Dad never did say who the father was, but he apparently knew the person, which made me curious. Why wouldn't he tell me? I wondered unless Mandy asked him to keep it to himself. Oh well, it didn't matter. It wasn't any of my business anyway.

Chapter Five
Patty

Mom dropped me off at school on her way to work the next day. I took a deep breath before entering the door that led into the gym where everyone hung out until we were allowed to go to our classes. I'd marked off today on both my calendars this morning. Fifty-five days until graduation and sixty days until Mattie's due date.

When I first discovered I was pregnant, I couldn't believe it was happening to me. I was a responsible person. I took my birth control pills faithfully and made Caleb Dalton, my former boyfriend, use a condom so I couldn't see how this had happened. My doctor reminded me that even though the pill was ninety-nine percent effective, there was always that one percent. Just one percent chance of getting pregnant and Caleb not wearing a condom one time would do it.

Although I was pretty vigilant about making sure Caleb wore a condom when we had sex, there had been a couple of times when we were partying that I was so smashed that I wouldn't have known if he did or not. Especially at the last party we went to as a couple. I didn't think that I had been drinking that much, but I woke up on my front porch the next morning and couldn't remember how I'd gotten home. That was when I started backing off drinking and taking pills at the same time. I'd recalled doing some Xanax that night, but even that shouldn't have made me black out.

It wasn't until school started back a few weeks later that I began hearing rumors that I'd participated in an orgy with a bunch of people that night. When I confronted Caleb about it, he'd just laughed and asked, "Don't you remember?"

Being the subject of rumors and speculation was not how I planned to start my senior year of high school, but that's the way things began. I've never been one to shy away from a bully, and I'd come pretty close to getting expelled from school for fighting a couple of times at the beginning of the school year. Principal Whipple finally stepped in and sorted out what was happening. Caleb and his group of friends were behind a lot of the bullying and rumors. I guess he just wanted to make sure that everyone knew he was done with me.

When I found out I was pregnant, I went straight to Caleb. He laughed in my face and said there was no way the baby was his. Mom went to Caleb's father, Eric Dalton, who is mayor of Riverton. Of course, he sided with Caleb and said that we would have to have a paternity test done. Eric had his lawyer draw up papers that said we could not tell anyone that Caleb was the baby's father unless the paternity test proved he was. I got so mad about the whole thing that I told all of them that if Caleb didn't want to be a part of the baby's life that he should sign his rights away and I would never tell anyone that the baby was his. So, that's what he did. I signed an agreement to never say Caleb was the father, and I thought we were done.

Caleb, however, has continued to bully me at school. He calls me names and intentionally bumps me in the halls. I don't have proof of the bullying and Caleb's dad has somehow tied Principal Whipple's hands over the matter. I try to avoid Caleb as much as possible and keep reminding myself that he will go away to college after high school and I probably won't see him again until our high school reunion.

This morning I made it to my locker without incident, but problems were waiting for me there. Destiny Black was standing a few lockers down from mine with a group of cheerleaders. Destiny has been Caleb's on and off again girlfriend since junior high. They were on again the last I heard.

When school started in August, Destiny staked her claim on Caleb again, after they had been broken up most of the summer and he had been dating me. At least I thought we were dating. Apparently, we were just screwing and partying according to him.

"You were just a summer fling," Destiny informed me when I'd confronted the two of them after Caleb dumped me.

I'd gotten Caleb alone later that same day and asked him if that was true. He'd just laughed and said, "Of course it's true. I can't be seen at school with an art nerd."

Today, Destiny turned and looked me up and down as I approached my locker. "My God! You're waddling."

"Fuck you," I said and opened my locker.

Destiny and her crew laughed, of course. I ignored them. Fifty-five more days, I kept saying in my head. It had become my mantra to remind myself every day how many more days until I was done with these assholes.

"I bet you that bastard you're carrying is Chet Barbar's," Ellie Deaton, a blonde bitch with perfect teeth said. "It'll come out looking like a small gorilla-like Chet."

I ignored her. She had been a bucktooth dog before she got a makeover from her plastic surgeon father and braces. I could have reminded her about that, but I wasn't taking the bait today.

My best friend, Daria Wilkins walked up to my locker. She looked at Destiny and her crew, and then turned to me. "Patty, you really need to talk to the janitor about cleaning the trolls out of the halls."

"I thought it was troll dung, that's why I'm ignoring them," I said and took my books out of my locker.

"Funny," Destiny snorted. "We'll see who's a worthless piece of shit when you're stuck in this tiny town with some loser."

"Fifty-five days," I said under my breath as Destiny, and the other cheerleaders walked off, shaking their asses and their pom-poms.

"I don't know if she realizes this, but Caleb will be right back here in this shit hole town working for his daddy after college. So it looks like she's going to be the one stuck here with a loser," Daria said as she watched them walk away, and then turned to me. "What did you say just now?"

"Fifty-five days," I said. "It's how long we have until graduation."

"Thank God!" Daria said.

We turned down the hallway that leads to our homeroom. "What did you do this weekend?" I asked.

Daria grinned and blushed. "Robby and I went camping at the Land Between the Lakes."

I turned and stared at her. "It was like thirty degrees Sunday morning."

"I know." Daria's smile widened. "Robby has a thirty below sleeping bag and an airtight tent. We were quite warm."

Shaking my head and thinking what a crazy fool she was, I said, "Yeah, I bet." Of course, if Daria were to get pregnant, her parents would insist on a wedding. A shotgun one if necessary. Daria's father is a farmer and a huge man. Her mother is a sweet, tiny woman, with black hair and eyes, who Daria took after. Both of her parents are very big on family responsibility. There would be no way some guy would get Daria pregnant and get away with not helping take care of the baby, at least financially.

I'm glad my mom didn't push for Caleb and me to get married. Even if Caleb Dalton's parents could have been won over to the idea, there was no way I could spend the rest of my life with that asshole. And I did not want his money because that would mean his family would have some say in how my baby was raised. As it stood now, none of them had any rights to the baby. In fact, only Caleb, his father, his mother, my mother, and I know that the baby I'm carrying is Caleb's. Even Daria doesn't know who the father of my baby is. I've told everyone else that the baby is some guy's that I partied with and I don't remember his name. Yeah, it looks terrible on me, but I know the truth, and that's all that matters.

Honestly, the only reason I agreed to go out with Caleb in the first place was because I was hell-bent on self-destruction. I knew in my heart that our affair would not last past the summer, but at the time I could not see past the pain of each day. By then, I was already taking Xanax. Daria's cousin, Billy started selling it to me when he was visiting for spring break last year. I had some money saved from when Mom and Dad would pay me for working for them, but I burned through it quickly. Caleb was looking for someone to have fun with, and he had the connections to get drugs and alcohol, so I became his party girl.

Daria didn't know about her cousin getting the pills for me until I was pregnant and had stopped taking drugs. She was furious and told her aunt about what happened. Apparently, the Xanax were Billy's mother's. It was a massive ordeal within Daria's family. Daria didn't speak to me for several months, but we made up after the first of this year.

"You're frowning," Daria noted.

"Just trying to remember if I brought my English homework. I'm pretty sure I picked it up off the kitchen table," I lied. I didn't want to get into it with Daria about my behavior over the summer. We were back on good terms with each other, and I wanted to keep it that way.

Chapter Six
Theresa

Mrs. Doan's gardens had gotten off to a good start, and then the rain hit. After the second day of hard downpours, I called Mandy McNeal and asked her if she wanted to meet with me to talk about her bed and breakfast. She agreed, and now I'm sitting outside this old brick house waiting for her. This job was going to be a real challenge to bring in for under fifty thousand dollars. Dad is confident I can do it, and I don't want to let him down.

It was raining too hard to walk around and take pictures, but I got a few shots with my phone from my truck. It would give me an idea of what to start with on the outside.

A few minutes later a small black Honda Civic pulled up behind me at the curb. Mandy got out and opened a large umbrella. I got out of my truck wearing my raincoat and pulled the hood over my head.

"Hi, Mandy," I said.

"Hi, Theresa. Thanks for calling me. I'd gotten busy at work and hadn't had a chance to call you." She motioned for me to follow her. "Come on. Let's get inside."

We both jogged to the front porch. Mandy quickly opened the front door. She closed her umbrella, shook off the water and stepped into the foyer with me right behind her. It was chilly in the house, so neither of us took off our coats.

We walked into the living room. "I know you're dad brought you out here to look at the house. So, do you think you can turn this into a decent bed and breakfast for fifty thousand, or less?"

"Honestly," I said, looking around the room. "It's going to be close. I've got some ideas and Dad said that you planned to do a lot of the simple labor, so that will keep the cost down." I walked over and looked at a large hole in the drywall. "Have you had the house checked for asbestos?"

"Yes," Mandy said. "Before I agree to buy it, I insisted the previous owner prove that it was either asbestos free, or lower the cost enough to cover having the asbestos removed." Then she smiled wryly, "But I also paid an inspector from the state to go over it. I didn't trust the seller that much."

"Good for you." Walking from the living room to the kitchen that had no appliances in it, I said, "We might have to replace a lot of the drywall."

"Yeah, I suspected that," Mandy said with a sigh. "According to the guy who I bought it from the electric wiring has been upgraded recently, but I'm not sure I'm buying that." She led me back to the living room. "Let's go upstairs and look around."

I followed her up the stairs, and we walked around the four large rooms. The walls up here were actually in decent shape. And then, I looked up at the ceiling and saw the large water stains. "Ought oh."

"Yeah, I know," Mandy said. "But it's supposed to have a new roof, and based on the fact

Page 33

that it doesn't appear to be leaking anywhere now, I think that is true."

"Is there an attic?"

"There's a small crawl space," Mandy said and took me to one of the bedrooms that had a pull-down ladder that led to the attic.

I pulled down the ladder and went up to have a look. She was right; it was just a small crawl space. There might be room for a small collection of boxes if someone wanted to use it for storage. I went up into the attic and crawled around on the beams checking for any dripping from the ceiling. At least the previous owner had not lied to her about the new roof.

When I came back down Mandy was looking at me expectantly. "Well?"

"It looks good, and as hard as it has been raining, I definitely think any leaks would be showing themselves."

I walked through each room, studying them for potential problems, and did a little math in my head. The more I thought about it, the more I felt that I could pull this off within her budget. There were things that she and her daughter would have to do to keep the costs down, but it was looking like the project could be finished for fifty thousand or less.

"So what kind of a time frame do you have on this?" I asked, taking the small spiral notebook I always carried out of my back pocket.

"Well," she said, drawing the word out a little. "This is the thing. My lease at the apartment I'm renting is up in a month. I don't want to renew it, and the landlord won't let me do a month to month. So I need a portion of this house somewhat livable in a month."

"Oh," I said with a heavy sigh. That would mean my team would have to work around Mandy and her daughter. Not the most comfortable circumstances for anyone. I looked around these rooms again. These would probably be the easiest to get ready, but they would need the kitchen and a bathroom available.

Mandy sensed my hesitation. "Let's go downstairs, and I'll tell you what I think we can do."

"Okay," I said and followed her down the stairs.

She took me to the kitchen. "I think that we can get the kitchen, bathroom, and this bedroom ready pretty quickly," she said walking into the bedroom closest to the kitchen. "We don't need a lot of room. Patty and I get along really well and can share a bedroom for a few weeks, but I do want to get the other downstairs bedroom fixed up before the baby comes."

I made notes in the notebook as she talked.

"I've ordered the appliances, but they won't be delivered until the kitchen is ready." She motioned to the cabinets. "I'm not worried about getting new cabinets. I think these can be used. I do want to get the walls repaired and make sure the electric is up to speed." She turned to look at me. "Do you guys have an electrician on staff?"

"Yes," I assured her and made a note to call Oscar, our head electrician as soon as I got back to the office.

"What about a plumber?"

"Yep," I said making another note.

"How soon could you give me a quote on doing these three rooms for starters?" Mandy asked, nervously brushing a strand of auburn hair away from her face.

I looked into her worried eyes and realized they were the same shade of hunter green as Patty's. "I'll try to have a preliminary quote done by the end of the day tomorrow. How does that sound?"

"Excellent," Mandy said, clearly relieved.

"I'm going to take some pictures with my phone. It helps me work out the plans if I can see what I need to do," I said and started taking pictures of the three rooms where we would begin working.

"Okay. If you need to take more pictures, Patty and I will be here this weekend. We're going to start cleaning the cabinets."

Nodding, I said, "I'll keep that in mind. I'm going to get back to the office and start working on this. Dad sent me your email address. Do you want me to email you the quote?"

"That will be great," Mandy said and walked with me to the front door. She picked up her umbrella and followed me out to the porch, locking the door behind us. "When you get ready to start I'll get you a key to the house."

"That would be great. Of course, I'll give it back once you guys start living here," I said and pulled my hood up over my head.

"Okay," she smiled. "It sounds like we have an initial plan."

"Yes, ma'am," I agreed.

Mandy put her hand on my arm. "Thank you for doing this, Theresa. Your dad speaks very highly of you, and I'm trusting you to do a good job."

"I'll do my best," I promised.

Chapter Seven
Patty

"I'm going with you to work on the new house," I said firmly.

"But, Honey, I'm going to have a kerosene heater going. The fumes might hurt the baby," Mom said.

I rolled my eyes. "Mother, many women over the centuries have been around different types of fuel, coal, oil, wood, and kerosene and their babies turned out just fine. I'm not going to be huffing the kerosene straight from the can. If anything the fumes from the bleach might be more harmful."

"Which is why you should stay home," Mom said as she loaded a plastic tub with cleaning supplies.

Putting my hands on my hips, I glared at her. "Are you meeting Richard Garland over there for a hookup? Is that why you don't want me to go?"

Mom quickly caught the bottle of cleaner that she almost dropped. "Patricia Marie! I am not meeting Richard!"

"Well?"

"Alright, fine!" Mom snapped. "Grab your coat. It's your baby. Put her at risk if you want."

Honestly, I just wanted something to do. It was Saturday. All my homework was done. Daria was with Robby. All of my other friends were doing stuff with their families or boyfriends, and I was bored out of my mind. I have hated our dank little apartment ever since we first moved into it. And, I want to be part of putting together the bed and breakfast.

When we got to the new house, Mom put me in the kitchen working on the cabinets. They weren't super dirty, but there was a brown film on them from where the previous occupants had been heavy smokers.

Mom wanted to strip the paint off the cabinets and get them down to the original wood and then stain the wood a pretty cherry color, but we wanted to get the grime off of them first.

While I was working in the kitchen, Mom started on the bathroom. She'd ordered a new toilet and shower for the downstairs bathroom. The upstairs bathroom was going to have a claw tub and a shower so the guests would have a choice.

That was going to be a big undertaking according to Mom. We might end up having to have new pipes for the entire house since the plumbing had not been updated in a very long time.

This house had originally been built when only the very rich had running water. Mom did a bunch of research when she started looking for a historical home to turn into a bed and breakfast. She had been able to get a fair amount of information about the family who built this house and the renovations they had done. The last two owners had used the house as a rental and had not bothered with any improvements.

It was kind of cool being in a house with so much history, and a little creepy. I wondered if any ghosts are lurking in the house.

I had my earbuds in and was listening to music while I was cleaning, so I didn't hear the newcomers until Mom came into the kitchen with them. Richard and Theresa Garland were standing next to the kitchen door when Mom called my name, and I turned around.

Taking out my earbuds, I said, "Hey."

"Good morning," Richard said with an easy smile.

"Hey," Theresa said, her dark eyes looking into mine for a second before she looked away.

Her gaze gave me a little bit of a chill. Not a cold chill, just something tickling my nerves. Weird.

"We're going to do some measuring, so we can determine how much drywall to order for the walls and ceiling. I'm getting ready to do a bulk drywall order, and I want to get what we need for this job included," Richard said as an explanation for them being there.

"I've got a plumber lined up to come here on Wednesday to install the toilet and shower in the bathroom down here," Theresa said. "Do you want to keep the vanity that's in there?"

"For now," Mom said. "Since it's our bathroom, I'm not worried about doing anything fancy right away. I just want it to be functional. I do want to replace the linoleum. Patty and I will probably do that ourselves."

"Okay," Theresa said. "Do you want me to put off the plumber, to give you time to put the linoleum down first?"

I put my earbuds in my pocket with my phone and followed the three of them to the bathroom down the hall from the kitchen. Standing in the doorway, I watched Theresa take her booted foot and press hard in several places where the toilet and the tub used to be.

"The floor's solid. There must not have been any problems with leaks in here," she noted.

"No," mom agreed. "I toyed with just removing this linoleum and leaving the wood floor bare, but then I imagined getting splinters while walking around in here barefoot."

"Theresa could put a coating on the floor if you wanted to do that," Richard said, moving close to Mom.

The warm look she gave him did not go unnoticed by Theresa, or me. In fact, Theresa turned to me and grinned knowingly. I returned the grin, mostly because her smile lit her face up in a way that made it impossible not to. Mom had told me the story about Richard and her dating in high school. It was obvious they still had feelings for each other.

I noticed that Theresa's hair was a little shorter than she had worn it in high school. Back then she'd had her dark brown hair in a ponytail most of the time, but you could tell it probably went to her shoulders when it was down. Now, her thick hair curled a little at her neck, and brushed the collar of her blue jean, button-up shirt. I envied her dark brown, almost black tresses. It was so much prettier than my dark auburn hair.

When I realized that I'd stared at her longer than I'd intended, I looked away and said, "We could probably have the linoleum in here by Wednesday if you decided that's what you want to do. We could go ahead and get it today. We'll need to roll it out and let it warm up. It wouldn't take us a few hours to get all this linoleum pulled up."

"That's a good idea," Mom said. "We are on a pretty tight schedule for getting the bathroom done. I think we could live with everything else the way that it is when we move in, but we definitely have to have the bathroom in working order."

"If you want, Theresa and I can help you today and tomorrow," Richard offered.

"I appreciate that Richard," Mom said, "but I can't afford to pay you to do the stuff we can do ourselves."

Richard smiled, changing his features from handsome, to stunning. No wonder Mom seemed to be falling for him all over again. Theresa had inherited her father's handsomeness; I noted as she smiled too.

"Yeah, Dad wanted to come over and offer a hand with some of this little stuff because we know you're on a time limit," Theresa said.

"I can't let you do that," Mom protested.

"Why not?" Richard asked, putting his hand on Mom's arm. "We've been friends for years, even if we haven't seen each other in a long time. Can't an old friend help you out?"

Mom stared at him for a long time and then turned to Theresa, "Are you sure? This is your business."

"Well, I'm expecting to do such a great job that you will tell all your friends about how great our company is, and I'm hoping you'll let me post a sign in your yard advertising that I'm the one doing the remodel," Theresa explained. "This is the first really big job I've done on my own, and I want to use it for promotional purposes. We'll be helping you move the project along by donating some of our time as friends, and the project getting done quickly will look good for our business."

Mom looked at me. "What do you think?"

"I don't think we should look a gift horse in the mouth," I said. "We could use the help."

Mom smiled and said, "She's right."

Richard and Theresa both beamed. "Let's do this," Richard said.

Theresa looked around and said, "Do you all not have some kind of heater to use?"

"We have a kerosene heater," Mom said and moved past all of us to the living room. "Shit. It's out of kerosene."

Theresa picked up the plastic gas can with the fuel in it. "I'll get this going again."

I watched as she opened the heater's tank and poured the kerosene inside. She expertly started the heater, for which I was glad because I was starting to get a chill. Mattie pressed her feet into my ribs, apparently in protest of the cold. I rubbed my lower ribs where she'd just kicked me.

"You okay?" Theresa asked, giving me a concerned look.

"Yeah. The baby was making her presence known," I said.

"Should you be here around these fumes and stuff?" she asked.

I rolled my eyes. "Yes. I'm fine."

"I tried to talk her out of coming," Mom said from the door.

"Yeah, and," I said nodding in Richard's direction, making Mom blush.

"What?" Richard asked.

"Come on," Mom said. "Let's go rip up some linoleum."

"What was that about?" Theresa asked.

I turned to her and grinned. "I accused her of not wanting me to come with her today so she could hook up with your dad, and low and behold here he is."

Theresa laughed out loud. "He tried to talk me out of coming too."

"Did he tell you about their history?" I asked.

Theresa smiled and nodded. "I already knew a little before he told me about them. It was one of the big fights Mother and he had when they were going through their divorce. She accused him of never getting over your mom," Theresa said.

"Well, I guess that might be true."

Theresa looked in the direction of the bathroom and nodded. "Yeah, I guess so."

"I'm going to get back to cleaning the cabinets. Working will help keep me warm," I said.

"True," she agreed. "I need to start doing some measuring, so we can get the drywall ordered. It saves us a lot of money when we can order in bulk."

I turned and headed for the kitchen. At the doorway, I stopped and watched her start measuring the living room. It was definitely going to need some new drywall. There were several holes, too many to patch. She looked like she knew what she was doing. Hopefully, she would be able to help keep the cost down. I turned away when I realized I was staring again. For some reason, I seem to be fascinated by her, and I have no idea why.

Chapter Eight
Theresa

Patty is quite energetic for a woman well into her pregnancy. We decided it was a waste of time for her to clean the outsides of the cabinets if Mandy wanted to sand them down and stain them. I started taking the cabinet doors off while Patty cleaned the inside of the cabinets. She was almost on my heels as she cleaned behind me.

Dad and Mandy ordered sandwiches for lunch, so we took a break around one o'clock. We all sat down in the living room on the floor. "I should have brought some camping chairs," Mandy said.

"It's getting about that time of the year," Dad said. "We will probably be getting our camping stuff out in the next week or so."

"So you still like to camp?" Mandy asked.

"Oh yes," Dad said. "Theresa and I usually start in April and go several times before it gets too warm, and then we'll take a break during the really hot months. We'll start again in late September and camp up until the end of December, depending on the weather."

"What about you guys?" I asked, wondering if Patty liked to camp.

"We didn't go any last year," Patty said. "I was being stupid, and it was just too hard without Dad."

Mandy sighed. "Yes, you were making some awful choices around this time last year. And yes, it was hard to imagine camping without Pat."

Dad reached over and patted Mandy's hand. "Well, maybe this year you guys can go with us."

"Maybe," Mandy said, looking at Patty, who shrugged.

"I guess if they don't mind a baby tagging along," Patty said.

"I don't think the baby going with us will be a problem," Dad said, smiling at Patty.

"Well, then, I'm in," Patty said. "I love camping, especially if there's fishing involved."

"We'll have to get some mosquito netting for the baby," I said.

"I bet you we could come up with a plan to make a little mosquito net tent for the baby," Dad said.

The rest of our time eating lunch was spent talking about where would be an excellent place to go camping in the next month before Patty had the baby. Someplace close to Paducah would be a good idea, just in case, Patty went into labor early.

Back in the kitchen a little while later, Patty started on the walls around where the refrigerator and stove would be going. Mandy wanted to paint the kitchen a warm yellow color. The kitchen currently was an stained off-white with lots of dings that would need some drywall mud. Patty was cleaning the sticky residue off the walls. When she finished the areas where the refrigerator and stove would be, she got a step ladder and started sweeping the cobwebs around the back door that led out to the back patio.

"Should you be climbing a ladder?" I asked.

Patty looked at me over her shoulder and rolled her eyes. "I'm fine."

She was making me nervous, so I started cleaning the walls close to her. I'm not sure what I would do if she did fall, but I could at least attempt to catch her.

Mandy came into the kitchen a few minutes later and hissed, "Patricia!" Scaring both of us.

Patty almost lost her balance, so I put my hands on her waist to stabilize her.

"Jesus Christ, Mom! You scared the shit out of me," Patty growled.

"I scared you? You scared me. You don't need to be up on a ladder like that," Mandy snapped.

Rolling her eyes as she had at me when I said something about her being on the ladder, Patty said, "I was fine until you shouted at me."

"I was keeping an eye on her," I told Mandy.

Mandy looked at me and then Patty, whose waist I was still holding on to, and raised an eyebrow. "Well, then, why don't you help her get down from there."

I let go of Patty's waist and took her hand as I helped her down from the ladder. Moving away from the wall and close to the doorway where Mandy was standing, we turned to look at our handy work. We'd scrubbed two full walls, including all the walls around the cabinets.

"You guys have done a great job," Dad said as he came into the room.

"Yes, you did," Mandy agreed giving Patty a side hug. "Sorry. I didn't mean to scare you. I just worry."

"I know," Patty said, hugging her mother back. "But, I'm not fragile."

"You may not be," Mandy agreed and then leaned down to kiss Patty's protruding belly. "But, Mattie is."

I laughed as I watched Patty shake her head. She was so damn cute when she was annoyed.

Patty put her hand on her stomach which growled loudly. "And she's hungry."

"Me too," Dad said. "How about we get cleaned up, and I take us all out to dinner?"

"Sounds good to me, but I'll pay for us," Mandy said.

"No arguments here," Patty agreed.

"Do we have anything that needs put away?" I asked moving to the wall Patty and I had been cleaning and gathering the rags and cleaning spray.

Mandy shook her head. "It's not supposed to get down to freezing tonight, so I think the cleaning supplies will be fine. Patty and I will be back here tomorrow to do some more."

"You might want to put the kerosene heater and kerosene up in one of the closets," Dad suggested.

"Yeah, that's a good idea," Mandy agreed.

"I'll take care of it," I volunteered, and left the kitchen to go to the living room. The heater was an excellent one that had the whole downstairs pretty warm. I turned it off and put the can of kerosene in the bathroom.

"I thought you were going to put it in a closet?" Patty asked.

I turned and looked at her. "I decided it might be too small a space with the fumes."

"That's true," she agreed.

"Where's Dad and Mandy?" I asked as I went back for the heater.

Patty followed me into the living room where I tested the heater to make sure it had cooled down. "There're outside discussing where we're going to eat. I'm just hoping they are going to let us go home and clean up."

"Me too." I nodded.

After I'd put the heater in the bathroom, we made sure the back door was locked. I followed Patty to the front door. She was still a small woman despite being six or seven months pregnant. Dad said Mandy hadn't said how far along Patty was, but she had mentioned the baby being due close to graduation. I couldn't imagine being pregnant and still in high school. Patty was so brave for staying and finishing. I'm not sure I would have been strong enough to do that. Of course, I had my own issues in high school and being forced out of the closet by Linda Dalton. I'd managed to make it through my senior year thanks to Dad and my friends, Frank and Darren who are also gay.

Patty seemed to be taking being pregnant in stride. Like telling her mother that she wasn't fragile. Most girls I knew in high school would have been laying around whining about how fat they were getting. I have to admit that I'm incredibly impressed with Patty's attitude.

"Richard wants to take us to Golden Corral," Mandy said when Patty and I approached them by the vehicles.

"Mmmm, a buffet," Patty said. "Sounds good to me. I'm starving."

"It does sound good," I agreed. "I'm craving fried chicken."

"So?" Dad turned to Mandy.

"I don't know about you paying for us, but I'm starved too," Mandy said.

Dad grinned, and I knew he would get his way. No matter what Mandy said, he wasn't going to let her pay for anyone's dinner. "Okay, we'll meet you at the Golden Corral on Memphis Road in thirty minutes."

"Alright, we'll see you there," Mandy agreed.

Dad was grinning as he got in the truck with me. "Pretty happy with yourself, aren't you?" I asked.

"I'm just pretty happy, kiddo. I'd missed Mandy. She was a good friend even when we weren't dating. I'm happy she has come back into my life. I don't know where it will lead, but I hope you're okay with me moving on," he said, turning to me and putting his hand on my shoulder.

I reached up and squeezed his hand. "It's been over two years, Dad. And you know Mom and I didn't have a good relationship, especially at the end. I want you to be happy, and if Mandy being in your life makes you happy, that's good enough for me."

"Thank you, baby girl," he said and put both hands on the steering wheel.

I looked out the side window and wondered how he would feel about me having a crush on his potentially reunited love's daughter. I'd thought Patty was pretty when she was a freshman in high school. Now, she was a senior about to graduate and more beautiful than ever. I doubted anything would come of it, though. Patty was apparently not gay.

Chapter Nine
Patty

I had a spring in my step coming into school Monday morning. Saturday had been a very productive day and having dinner with Theresa and Richard had been fun.

I remember Theresa being a bit of a jock when she was here. She'd played basketball, and I'd seen her in the art room a few times. We'd never spoken, other than the occasional greeting. But I always remember thinking she seemed nice, and it turns out she is.

When I'd seen her at the Chinese restaurant that first time with Mom, there had been a memory tickling my brain. It hit me yesterday what that memory was. It was from when the news had come through the school Theresa's senior year that she'd been outed as a lesbian. I had been a little surprised. I guess I don't know what I thought a lesbian should look like, but I didn't associate Theresa with that description. At school, she dressed in clothes that were with the current style, jeans with holes in the knees and t-shirts with cool sayings on them, or polo shirts. In the winter, she wore a lot of long-sleeved t-shirts or long-sleeved polo shirts. Now that I think about it, she did look a little butch, and I apparently paid more attention to her than I realized.

It had been a big deal at our small school at the time. Linda Dalton had basically accused Theresa of sexually assaulting her. Later, a story came out that Linda had been the one to initiate their affair. The two of them had been caught making out in Linda's bed at the Dalton house by Linda's younger brother, Caleb. The same Caleb who was the father of my baby.

Linda had been shipped off to live with relatives in a different town, and Theresa had been left to deal with the fallout. She'd suffered through some severe harassment from Caleb and some of the guys who had been friends with the Dalton family. For the most part, everyone else took the news in stride. There were a few people who seemed determined to make Theresa's life hell. I remember that there were even a few other kids who came out as gay in support of Theresa so she wouldn't feel so alone.

The school had hushed the story up and dealt with the bullies bothering Theresa, and anyone else who had come out pretty quickly. I'd never figured out what happened, but I always suspected it was Caleb's father wanting the story to die down because he was running for mayor of Riverton that year.

This year, there are four kids in my class who are out and proud. All four of them are friends of mine. They are either in my art class or are part of the drama club. I think that's why I'm so comfortable with Theresa, although I found her over-protectiveness at the house this weekend a little annoying.

We got a lot done over the weekend at the new house thanks to Theresa and her father coming back out to help on Sunday. There was still plenty of work for Mom and me to do, but we'd reached a point in a few of the rooms where it was time to bring in the professionals. Mom and I were going back tonight to start knocking down the drywall in the living room. "Hey girl!" Daria called as she approached me. Daria was wearing a sea green long sweatshirt over purple yoga pants today. Yoga pants or leggings were all the Daria wore. She hasn't worn regular blue jeans since junior high, which I think is weird because I love my blue jeans. I hate these maternity pants. They look stupid, and I have to wear oversized maternity shirts over them. Just a few more months, I remind myself.

"Hey, yourself," I said as I walked over to her locker.

"You sounded tired last night when I called," Daria said.

"I was. We spent Saturday and Sunday working on the new house," I said and leaned against her locker.

"I want to help when you start painting. I think that will be fun," Daria said and got out the books she needed for the next couple of classes.

"Yeah, I'm looking forward to that part," I said. "At first, it is just going to be simple colors, but after I have the baby, I'll be able to paint my room the way I want, and I want to add some flowers and butterflies to the walls."

We turned and started walking toward homeroom. I saw Caleb coming toward us and clenched my fist. I wanted to punch that son-of-a-bitch in the face every time I saw him.

"Look, guys," Caleb called to his friends. "It's a whale moving through the halls."

His friends laughed, and I took out my phone. I looked down at the screen as he approached, turned the camera on and hit the record button. I didn't raise it up until Caleb moved into my path. I turned to step away from him, and he caught my wrist and grabbed my phone.

"Hey, give that back," I shouted as loud as I could, hoping to attract a teacher's attention.

Caleb hit the end button, not realizing he was automatically sending the recording to my Google Drive. "I don't want my picture on your phone, bitch," he spat at me and deleted the record.

I saw Mr. Jacobs, one of the math teachers coming down the hall, and shouted at Caleb, "GIVE ME MY PHONE!"

Mr. Jacobs stepped between Caleb and me. "Is there a problem?"

"Yes, this cow was taking my picture," Caleb said and threw the phone at me.

I almost caught it, but it fell to the floor and the screen shattered.

"Mr. Dalton, you will be accompanying me to the principal's office," Mr. Jacobs said.

"No, I won't," Caleb said, turned and walked away.

"That's what he thinks," Mr. Jacobs said, his face turning red. He leaned down and picked up my phone. "Miss McNeal, please come with me to the office. We're going to file a report with the school's police officer." He looked around noting who was standing there watching. "I think we have enough witnesses to prove Mr. Dalton intentionally damaged your phone."

Caleb's friends had hurried after him, but several of the other students standing around said they would be a witness.

I'd noticed that Caleb's popularity had waned this year because he had become a horrible bully, especially with the underclassmen athletes.

Daria walked with me to the principal's office. The school's police officer, Officer Craig just happened to be standing at the front desk when Mr. Jacobs led Daria, several other witnesses and me into the office.

"Excellent," Mr. Jacobs said when he saw Officer Craig. "Miss McNeal wants to file personal property damages against Caleb Dalton. These other students are witnesses."

Officer Craig turned to me and rested his hands on his duty belt. "What happened?"

"Caleb was approaching me, calling me a whale. I was trying to move away from him, but he kept coming in my direction. My lawyer told me to try to record anytime Caleb gets into my personal space because I've already complained about the bullying, but I haven't had proof," I explained.

"Yes, I'm aware of the bullying complaints against Mr. Dalton," Officer Craig sighed. "So what property did he damage?"

I held up my phone and showed him the cracked screen. "He broke my phone."

Mr. Jacobs spoke up. "All of these witnesses can testify that Mr. Dalton took the phone from Miss McNeal and then threw it back at her. She couldn't catch it because of how hard he threw it and it fell to the floor and shattered."

"He did that because I recorded him in my face," I said.

Now, Principal Whipple and Vice Principal Callous had come out of their offices to see what was going on. Mr. Jacobs said, "Mr. Dalton refused to come to the principal's office with me. I know the seniors only have a few weeks left, but they still have to treat the teachers and their fellow students with respect."

"Absolutely," Principal Whipple said sternly. He turned to Officer Craig. "Would you mind going to Mr. Dalton's class with Vice Principal Callous and myself? Mr. Dalton will be coming to the office with us."

"Yes, sir," Officer Craig said.

I knew Officer Craig was probably tired of hearing about the crap going on between Caleb and me. But, Caleb wouldn't stop screwing with me, and I am not going to put up with it. I don't give a damn that his father is the mayor, or that he's already gotten a scholarship to go to the University of Kentucky to play football. I just want him to leave me alone.

I think part of Caleb's problem is that he's never had a girl stand up to him. Most of the girls in our class still fall all over themselves when he comes around with his cronies. I get it. He is handsome and well-built, and when the girls are fawning all over him, he acts like this super guy. But, when someone crosses him, he becomes a total jerk to them. Of course, the fact that I've accused him of fathering my child has put me on the top of his list of people who have pissed him off. I don't get why he cares anymore. He signed his rights away, so my child is no longer his problem or his business. But, I think he wants me to cow down to him, and that will happen over my dead body.

An hour later, I found myself still sitting in the principal's office. Now, my mother, our lawyer; Mr. Reed, Eric and Caleb Dalton, Mr. Dalton's lawyer; Mr. Charleston, Officer Craig, and Principal Whipple were all there.

Mr. Whipple was sitting behind his desk with his hands folded in front of him. He looked around the room at everyone. "We only have a few more weeks until school will be out for you two."

"Forty-nine days," I supplied.

Frowning at me, Mr. Whipple repeated, "We just have a few more weeks of school. I don't understand why the two of you keep picking at each other, but it needs to stop."

"She needs to stop telling people I'm the father of that kid," Caleb grumbled. "And she needs to stay away from me."

"Stay away from you?" I shouted. "I avoid you as much as I possibly can. You're the one that seeks me out. And I haven't told anyone about you being this baby's father since you signed your rights away, not even Daria, so if anyone is saying that, it isn't me."

"That's enough," Mr. Whipple snapped.

"It's unfortunate that you to have classes in the same area of the school, but it is something you two will have to deal with. If you see each other in the hall, I want you both to move as far away from each other as you can," Officer Craig said. "Based on the bullying complaints that have already been filed, Mr.

Dalton has been warned repeatedly to stay away from Miss McNeal. I realize sometimes here at school it is unavoidable. But, you should be able to keep twenty to thirty feet between each other."

"I agree," Mr. Whipple said. He turned to Caleb and held up my phone. "You destroyed this young lady's phone in front of several people, and I expect you to make reparations."

"I'll pay for a new phone for Patty," Eric Dalton said curtly and glared at his son. "You will follow the guidelines set up here for you. I don't want to be brought down here again over this petty crap, Caleb."

"Yes sir," Caleb mumbled.

"What was that," Eric shouted in Caleb's ear.

"Yes, sir," Caleb said louder.

"Now," Mr. Whipple said, "I'm glad both parents brought their lawyers to this meeting because I want as many witnesses as possible to what I'm about to say." He turned to Caleb. "Mr. Dalton, you have the most to lose if you do not comply with these rules. If you continue to harass Miss McNeal, if I hear of you bullying anyone between now and the end of the school year, I will forward your disciplinary record to the recruiters at the University of Kentucky. I don't think you were that high on their pick list that they will be interested in dealing with someone who has disciplinary problems."

"You can't do that!" Eric Dalton raged.

"Yes, I can, Mr. Dalton, and I will," Principal Whipple said firmly. "Miss McNeal is not the only student who has complained about your son's behavior. Most of them are too afraid of him to file official charges, but I've been keeping a list of the complaints. I'm not going to put up with this behavior any longer. I have over five hundred students, and your son has been afforded a lot of the privileges a star sports player are given at this school, but I will not tolerate a bully no matter how many games he's won. Are we clear?"

"Yes," Eric Dalton said and stood. "We're done here. Get up, Caleb. You're going home." He turned to mom and me and sneered before saying, "I'll make sure you have no more problems with Caleb."

After the Daltons and their lawyer left the office, Principal Whipple turned to me. "I sincerely hope you are not doing anything to provoke Caleb intentionally."

"Principal Whipple, I promise you that I try to avoid him. He's the one who seeks me out. And there are only a handful of people who know that Caleb fathered my child, but he's signed his rights away, so as far as I'm concerned, he has no role in my child's life, or in my life. His problem with me is that I won't back down and he can't stand it."

"Well, hopefully, now that we've brought this to his father's attention, things will get better." He smiled then and said, "As you said, we only have forty-nine days of school left. Don't think students are the only ones counting the days."

I smiled too. "I have no doubt."

Mom let me go home with her. She told the principal that she thought I'd had enough drama for one day and needed the rest. I was so happy she did that. I didn't want to go through the rest of the day knowing that Caleb would sic Destiny on me in his stead.

We went straight to the new house where Theresa and her crew were working. They were tearing down the drywall in the bedroom Mom and I will share at first. Her guys and she were hard at work.

Mom had this week off from work so she could take care of things at both the house and the apartment. At first she was going to take me home, but I told her I needed to do something to work off my anger, so she took me to the new house with her.

We went to work on the kitchen. Mom took the doors from the cabinets outside and started putting the stripper on them, and I started patching holes in the walls with drywall mud.

Theresa came in about an hour after we got there and stood in the doorway of the kitchen observing my handy work. "You're pretty good with that knife," she said.

"I spent a lot of time working with my dad. There were a lot of small jobs he didn't want to pay a crew to work on, so he would have Mom and me help him."

"He trained you well," Theresa said.

"Thank you," I said quietly, suddenly missing Dad.

"It had to have been hard losing your dad," she said.

I nodded. "It was. It still is sometimes."

"Well, they say time heals all wounds," Theresa said softly. "I'm not completely sure about that, but I suppose the pain does lessen with time."

"What about you? Do you miss your mom?" I asked. I didn't know the whole story about Richard and Theresa's mom's divorce, but Mom told me it had been very hard on Theresa.

"Nope," Theresa said firmly. "And I doubt she or my brother miss me."

I stopped and looked at her, surprised. "Really?"

She stood there looking at me for several seconds, like she was deciding about saying something, but then changed the subject. "I'm going to put some plastic up to block this room off from the other rooms where we're going to start cutting the drywall up into manageable pieces to throw in the dumpster. "I'm not sure how much of the dust will get in here, but you might want to think about going somewhere else for a few hours."

"I'm almost done. There are just a few more dings on the wall over here," I said pointing in the direction of the back wall. After that, I'll get Mom to take me home for a while."

"That would be great," Theresa said and smiled with a nod toward my stomach. "I don't think Miss Matilda needs to be breathing in a bunch of dust."

I smiled at her. "No, she doesn't."

Theresa reached out with her hand and gently pulled a piece of drywall mud out of my hair. "Looks like you got a little carried away with the mud."

"Yeah, I was in a rhythm slapping it on the walls. It's okay. It washes out," I said, but I liked the way she had carefully pulled the sticky substance out of my hair. There was something about her that seemed so gentle and sweet. Her presence always made me feel a little warm. It was kind of strange but nice.

"I'm going to go get the plastic and start putting it up. You finish so you can get out of here before it gets messy," she said, turned and went back to the other room with her guys.

I watched her walk away and thought she had a very confident strut. What she'd said about her brother and mother made me curious and a little sad. I'd hate to have family out there who I didn't think missed me. Maybe Mom knew the whole story. I'll have to ask her later.

Chapter Ten
Theresa

Patty has no right looking so damn cute putting drywall mud on the walls. I'm not sure what possessed me to take the drywall mud out of her hair. It was like my hand reached out of its own accord. Shaking off my thoughts of Patty McNeal, I returned to my guys and asked John to help me put up the plastic over the door leading into the kitchen.

Mandy had knocked down a lot of the drywall in the living room earlier in the day. By the end of the day, we'd finished ripping out all the drywall in the two downstairs bedrooms, living room and bathroom. Tomorrow I'll have our electrician take a look at the wiring. It looked okay for the most part but better safe than sorry.

I'm going to send my guys to Mrs. Doan's house in the morning because it's not supposed to rain and we'll have to wait for the drywall to be delivered before we can do anything else downstairs.

I'm very impressed with how hard Patty and Mandy are working on this project. Granted it was taking some money from me, but I understood that Mandy's budget was very tight. She hoped to have the bed and breakfast up and running in six months. That was a pretty tall order, but at the rate that they were working, it might just be possible.

When I got home, Dad asked me about the day. I told him how far we'd gotten with the downstairs.

We started working on dinner together. It was something he and I had always been good at even when we lived with Mom and Jonah.

"What's wrong?" Dad asked when I'd gotten quiet.

"Patty asked me if I missed Mom and Jonah today," I answered.

"What did you say?" He stopped turning the hamburgers and looked at me.

"I said no, and that I didn't think they missed me either." I kept cutting the tomatoes and he went back to the hamburgers.

"I'd like to think they miss us," he said quietly.

"You know I'm sorry for what happened," I said.

"It wasn't your fault, Theresa," Dad said. "There had been problems for a long time. Your mom was never a happy person."

"I always felt like she never wanted me," I said, and swiped at a stray tear. I promised myself I'd never cry over that woman again, but sometimes the pain of how much hatred she'd shown me would break me down. Patty asking about her today seemed to have re-opened that wound a little bit. I was being empathetic for her pain of losing her father, and she'd try to reach out to me too. Letting someone know how much my mother had hurt me was hard for me. Even Dad didn't truly know the depth of the pain that woman had caused me.

"That's not true," Dad said, turning to me again, but I could see that he wasn't so sure either.

"It doesn't matter," I said and started cutting the cucumbers a little harder than necessary. "I'm just sorry that she hurt you over me."

Dad put down the spatula and took me by both arms, forcing me to drop the knife and look at him. "She hurt me because she hurt you. I had known for a long time that she was a selfish, mean-spirited woman. But when she said those horrible things to you and told you to leave, I wasn't going to stand by and let her do that to you. She was wrong, and one day she will be sorry she threw us out of her life."

"She threw me out of her life, Dad. You didn't have to leave," I said, tears falling freely now.

"Yes, I did," he said firmly. "There was no way I was going to let you be thrown out on the streets on your own. You are my daughter, and I will never let anyone hurt you and abuse you like your mother did, ever again. You understand me?"

I nodded, put my arms around him, and laid my head on his broad shoulder. He wrapped his arms tightly around me and held me close. Stroking my hair, he asked, "I'm sorry you still have all this pain. Did Patty asking about them bring all this out?"

"I was watching Patty work at the house today, and she was doing a great job with the drywall mud. When I said something to her about it, she said her dad had taught her. She spoke of him with such warmth, and it made me realize how lucky I am to have you. I would be so devastated if something happened to you. I might even have made the kind of mistakes Patty did," I said.

Dad pulled back and looked me in the eye. "Nothing's going to happen to me, and I don't think you would make those same mistakes. You don't even like beer, let alone hard alcohol, or men."

I smiled slightly. "True, but maybe the pills. I hear Xanax makes you pretty loopy."

Dad cupped my face in his hands and kissed my forehead. "I'm going to burn the hamburgers." He handed me a paper towel to wipe my face.

"Sorry, must be that time of the month. You know I'm not usually this emotional," I said.

IIe made a sour face. "More than I need to know."

Laughing I said, "Sorry."

"Let's talk about something else," he said. "I talked to Mandy about going camping. What do you think about the four of us going out to Kentucky Lake this weekend?"

"It's not going to be too cold, is it?" I asked and went back to cutting the vegetables.

"It's going to get down into the forties, but up into the sixties during the day. We'll take the camper, so it won't exactly be roughing it," he said.

My hand stopped moving as I saw the four of us in the camper. Mandy and Dad on one side and me and Patty on the other. Shaking off my thoughts of being snuggled up to Patty under a sleeping bag, I said, "Sounds good to me."

"You and Patty seemed to have hit it off pretty good, so I thought it should be fun. Mandy said Patty wasn't kidding when she said she loves to fish. You and I both love to fish too. Mandy's not that excited about catching the fish, but she said she'd cook whatever we catch," Dad said and took the hamburgers out of the skillet and laid them on the paper towel covering a plate.

"You know, you've told me the highlights of the story of you and Mandy, but I think you should give me the details," I said as I set the plate of vegetables on the table.

Dad took the french fries out of the oven and scooped them out into a large bowl. "There's not much more to tell. Mandy and I started dating our sophomore year in high school. I was a football player, and she was an artist. We should have had very little in common, but both of our fathers were in construction. Her father worked for mine. But, God, she was so beautiful. That rich auburn hair and those green eyes were like magnets for me when we were in the halls together.

"Back then, going to the high school football game was the highlight of everyone's week. Mandy always came with her friends. I'd watch for her in the stands. When football season ended, I started spending more time hanging out after school with the theater kids so I could be around Mandy. She got me to help them build and paint the sets. I just totally fell in love with her."

We both sat down and started filling our plates. "So what happened?" I pressed.

"My senior year, I got pretty full of myself. I was the lead running back, making the most important plays of each game. I was starting to make plans to play football in college. Some recruiters were looking at me." He sighed heavily. "I started thinking I was too good for a girl whose father worked for my father's company."

My mouth hung open with my sandwich stopped halfway to my face. This was not the man I knew. I couldn't imagine my dad ever being that way. He was always so humble about his upbringing.

"I know, it sounds wrong to me too, but I was eighteen and thought I had the world by the tail," Dad said and looked off into the distance past me. "I broke up with Mandy. I was so stupid, so selfish. I hurt her, but I wanted someone who looked better on my arm in my family's social circles. I started talking to your mom. She had been dating Eric Dalton, the quarterback of our football team for a couple of years and they had just broken up. Kind of for the same reason, Eric had started dating Betsy Clapboard, the head cheerleader. Your mom came from the same kind of money Eric did, but she wasn't a part of anything special at school, like sports. She was just a pretty girl who was popular. Since Eric was the quarterback on our winning football team, he decided Betsy would fit his image better. Of course, Betsy had been after Eric for a while, and she was one of those girls who got what they wanted."

I watched my father's face twist into an angry mask.

"I hadn't planned on dating your mother after I went to college. I'd been accepted to Louisville's football team, and I planned to focus on school and playing football, but your mother wasn't going to let me go that easily."

"Is that when she told you she was pregnant with me?" I asked.

"Yes," he said quietly. "We got married, I started college and played football. It was rough. I was barely passing my classes. Dealing with your mother was hard. At the time I wasn't sure if I wanted to work for my dad, so I thought it was best to get an education in case I decided to do something else." He laughed bitterly. "There was never an option though. Your mother wanted to maintain a certain lifestyle, and I could only do that working for my dad. I quit school and Dad gave me a foreman job with the company. That made your mom happy."

"Didn't you like working for Grandpa?" I asked.

"I did. My father was a good man. Both of my parents were good people, and they both saw through your mother's facade. She wanted me for the money my family had, I don't know if she ever really loved me, maybe at first," Dad said.

"So did you guys fight from the beginning? I know you fought for as long as I can remember," I said.

"I guess so," he said and began putting his hamburger together. "Things got bad when we hired Pat as a subcontractor. Your mom came out onto the job one day, saw Mandy and flipped out. I tried to explain to her that Mandy was there working with her husband, Pat, but she wouldn't hear it. She wanted me to fire him. That's when my dad got involved. There was no way he was going to let your mother have me get rid of one of our best subcontractors."

"Was that the first time you'd seen Mandy since high school?" I asked.

He nodded. "When Mandy came out to the job with Pat, it was the first time I'd seen her since we'd graduated." He smiled. "She looked happy. We talked one day on a job when Pat was gone. She said she'd forgiven me. After I told her how things were with your mother, she'd laughed and said that it was karma. I think she was right."

"So you guys became friends again?" I bit into my sandwich and watched Dad nod sadly.

"Yeah, Pat was such a great guy. We often went out for a beer or dinner with Mandy. I'd always ask your mother to come, but she refused." He chewed on a french fry before continuing. "When she got pregnant with your brother, I felt it was her next trap. After she had you, she'd said she didn't want another child. So when she told me she was pregnant with Jonah, I knew she'd done it on purpose.

"When your mom told me she was pregnant with you, I thought you were an accident. Deidre acted furious about being pregnant, but she used her condition to keep me. He smiled. "When you were born, you stole my heart the second I laid eyes on you. You were my daughter, and I knew it right from the start. You had dark hair and eyes like mine. And there was something about the way you looked at me when I held you right after you were born. It was like that thing from that vampire movie. You know when they were talking about the baby imprinting on the werewolf?"

I burst out laughing. "You mean Twilight?"

"Yeah, it was the next to the last one, or the last one, when the baby was born, and she and the werewolf had the imprinting thing," he said.

My father had watched every one of the Twilight movies with me, and I didn't think he'd been paying attention, but I guess he was. "Actually, it was

Jacob who imprinted on Esme, but I get what you're saying. It's why we've always had a special bond."

"Yes, and your mother hated it. Once she got over being pregnant and had a little girl, she wanted so badly to turn you into a little debutante, but you were having no part of it." He laughed. "She would get so mad because she'd go to all this trouble to make you up and you'd have yourself turned into a mess five minutes later."

I laughed with him. It hadn't been funny at the time because my mother would often slap me when I didn't do what she wanted. "I guess she gave up when I started refusing to wear dresses."

"Yeah, but she had her precious boy," Dad said. "You know, your brother and I never had a bond. She would never allow it, and I knew in my heart she had gotten pregnant with Jonah so she could use him as a tool against me. It worked. She would whine about not being able to handle both of you so I would rush home after work to take care of you while she dealt with your brother. I don't know what she thinks is going to happen after he graduates from college, but he's not coming to work for me, and I'm not supporting him."

"That's probably why he will never graduate," I mused. "He knows he'll have to get a real job."

"He says he wants to get a doctorate in business, but I'm not paying for ten years of college," Dad said.

I smiled. "Aren't you glad I decided I would rather work than go to school?"

"Yes," he said lifting his tea and toasting. "To my girl, who is so much like her father. Thank God!"

"Cheers," I said and touched his glass laughing.

"Whoa, enough family talk," he said. "Tell me what you plan to do next at Mandy's house."

We spent the rest of the evening talking about Mandy's house and my plans for the next couple of weeks. I was confident we would have the downstairs ready for Mandy and Patty to move in before the end of April when they had to be out of their apartment. I was pretty sure we'd have a lot of the upstairs done too. Then, our focus would move to the outside. Mandy has a pretty specific garden plan in mind. It was going to take at least three weeks to put together, depending on the weather.

Later, when I was in bed, I realized how happy I was that Dad and I had talked about Mom. I was glad he understood how she had made me feel, and I was glad he didn't blame me for their split up.

Jonah was definitely her son, but he was my brother. We talked occasionally but not because he missed me. He usually just wanted to brag about how great his life was, like the fact that he was dating some girl whose family was loaded. I'm sure that made Mother happy. Not once during any of the conversations Jonah and I had since Dad and I moved out of the house did he mention Mom asking about me. I had no doubt she would never forgive me for not being her perfect daughter. That was okay. I had Dad, and I know his love for me is unconditional.

Chapter Eleven
Patty

I don't think I could be any more excited about going camping if I tried. I was so ready to get away from Riverton, even if it was only for a weekend. I told my doctor about us going camping, and she said everything was fine with Mattie. There wasn't any reason why I should worry about being out of town.

Mom was probably more worried than I was. She made sure we had everything necessary should I go into labor out in the woods. The packing list, which should have been a lot shorter included, several gallons of sterile water, extra blankets and towels, a heating pad, plus three or four outfits for each of us.

When Theresa and Richard got to our apartment and helped us start loading our car, Theresa assessed all the baggage and asked, "Are we going for a weekend or a month?"

"Shush," Mom admonished. "I just want to be prepared."

I turned to Theresa and said, "She's worried I'm going to go into labor out in the woods."

Theresa's eyes widened and she asked, "Are you already having contractions?"

"No, I'm fine," I laughed.

She looked relieved, but still studied my stomach as if the baby were going to jump out and grab her. I patted her on the arm and laughed again as

I grabbed one of the bags and put it in the back seat of the car.

Richard opened the trunk of our car and saw the sterile water. He looked over at Mom, who was loading suitcases in the back seat. "You know they have water hookups out there, right?"

Mom glared at him. He shut the trunk and mumbled, "Never mind."

In less than a half an hour, we were on the road to Kentucky Lake. Richard had already made reservations for the weekend, so all we had to do was get there and get set up.

Mom and I listened to music and talked about the house and the baby on the way to the lake. It took about an hour and a half to get there, but the time passed quickly.

Theresa and her team were moving along very quickly with the house. Mom was sure we were going to be able to start moving a few pieces of furniture into the house by the end of next week. I am excited about getting out of that tiny apartment. Next week, I'll be at the house every evening with Mom pushing the project further along.

The plumber had been out this week, so the downstairs bathroom and the kitchen sink were in working order. He'd run the pipes for the upstairs bathroom, but he would wait for Theresa to finish the upstairs before he would install the tub, shower, and toilet.

As far as I was concerned, now that we had the electricity turned on and running water, I was ready to move in, but Mom said we had to wait until next weekend.

We pulled up next to the campsite and watched Richard back up the camper with Theresa guiding him.

"She's very pretty," I commented to Mom, "but sometimes she can act like a guy."

Mom laughed. "Yeah, she's definitely got the tomboy thing going on."

Once the camper was set up, Theresa started a fire in the pit and the grill while Richard and Mom put together some hamburgers to cook on the grill. I sat next to the fire pit and watched Theresa get the fire going. I noted that she had long fingers and strong hands. I'd noticed how big her hands looked before, but I found myself fascinated with watching them tonight.

Theresa caught me staring at her and raised an eyebrow at me before looking at her fingers. "Do I have something on my hands?" she asked.

"No, I was just noticing how long your fingers are," I said.

She shrugged. "Both of my parents have big hands and long fingers."

I looked at my small hand. "I got Mom's hands. Dad's were much bigger than hers."

Smiling, Theresa reached over and pulled on one of my fingers. "Yes, you have tiny hands."

"What are you two talking about?" Mom asked when she brought out the hamburger patties to put on the grill.

"Hand size," Theresa said.

"She has big hands for a girl," I said.

"She has big hands period," Richard said as he came out of the camper packing a cooler. "Even as a little girl, her hands were big. He put the cooler next to the picnic table, took out a jug of sweet tea, and held up one of his own large hands. "She gets it from me. That's why I was a good receiver in football, and she was a good basketball player." He adjusted some items in the cooler and then set the plate of hamburger patties inside. "That'll keep them cold until we're ready."

I turned and looked out over the lake that was close to our camp. It was so big. It almost seemed like an ocean. Mom and I haven't been to this area since Dad died and I was looking forward to fishing early in the morning.

Theresa followed my gaze. "We have a spot down by the shoreline here," she said pointing to the water. "This is our usual camping spot, so we've taken some logs and rocks and made a nice sitting area by the shore."

"Awesome," I said. "I can't wait to get a line cast out there."

"Yep, first thing in the morning we'll go down and do some fishing before breakfast," Richard said.

"And if we get lucky, we might have fresh fish for breakfast," Mom said.

Before long Theresa had the fire roaring, which was perfect because it was chilly. Richard cooked the hamburgers, and we sat at the picnic table talking about fishing and camping. Richard and Theresa had always camped alone because Theresa's mother and brother didn't want to go. The camper had been Richard's father, Ted's, who had also been an avid fisherman and camper.

I teared up when Richard talked about how his father had gotten arthritis real bad and had to quit working, and then died of a heart attack. His mother, Sally was living in an assisted living facility in Bowling Green, where Richard's older sister, Nancy lived.

Mom talked about her parents living in Paducah and Dad's parents living in Florida. "They are all coming in for Patty's graduation," Mom said. "Pat's Mom and Dad are going to stay until the baby's born, so hopefully she'll be on time."

As if on cue, Mattie stuck a foot in my rib, making me groan with pain. "She says she'll be on time."

Everyone laughed.

I was getting cold and tired around nine-thirty, so I said, "Do we have the sleeping arrangements mapped out? I'm about ready for bed."

"Yep," Theresa said and stood. She held out her hand to me and pulled me to my feet. Going ahead of me into the camper, Theresa said, "You and Mandy will sleep over here." She put her hand on a thin bed in the front of the camper that was covered with a dark comforter. "Uh oh," she said pulling her hand away and looking at it. "That's wet." She lifted the comforter and felt the mattress. "Well, shit, that's wet too."

She went to the other side of the camper and tested the bed at that end. The shaking of her head told me that it was wet too. She went to the camper door and called out, "Dad, you need to come look at this. Both of the beds are wet."

"What?" Richard jumped up from his chair and came into the camper. He felt both beds and the cushioned chairs at the table. "Damn."

"What's the matter?" Mom asked.

"That last big storm we had. A tree branch fell on top of the camper. I didn't think it had done any damage, but there's apparently a big leak somewhere," Richard said with his hands on his hips. Shaking his head at the disaster, he said, "I guess we'll have to go to the lodge and see if they have any rooms."

"No, we don't," Mom said. "We've got a tent, a blow-up mattress and sleeping bags in the trunk of my car." She grinned sheepishly. "But they're behind the water."

Richard laughed out loud. "Are you sure we can all fit on the mattress?"

"It's a king," Mom said. "It might be a little tight, but we'll have more body heat to keep us warm."

He turned to look at Theresa and me. "Well, if you two don't care."

"I don't care," I said. "I'm ready to pile up anywhere."

"Okay, let's do this," Theresa said and led the rest of us out of the camper.

We all pitched in on getting the tent out of the car and getting it up. Mom and Richard blew the mattress up while I sat next to the dying fire that Theresa stirred. "You think we should let them sleep next to each other?" she asked.

"No, way," I said. "We don't want to encourage any hanky-panky while we're in the tent with them."

"Yeah, that would be gross," Theresa agreed.

"Totally," I said.

"Okay," Mom said. "It's ready."

"I probably should be on the outside since I'm going to have to go to the bathroom every few hours," I said.

"I'll have to go too," Mom said. "Now, that I had tea this late, I'll be up and down too."

Richard and Theresa looked at each other and shrugged. "That's fine," Theresa said. "I don't usually wake up once I'm out."

"Me either," Richard said.

In the end, Richard and Mom did end up sleeping next to each other, and Theresa slept next to me. After everyone was settled in, Richard said, "I left the camper door unlocked so you can get in to go to the toilet. I've got the heat on too. I'm hoping it will dry the mattresses overnight and we can sleep in there tomorrow night."

"Thank you," I said, happy I wasn't going to have to try to squat in the woods or make my way to the bathroom several campsites away.

The heavy-duty sleeping bag and Theresa's body heat helped lull me into sleep pretty quickly, but as was typical, I woke a few hours later having to go to the bathroom. The camper was super warm, but it was chilly outside, and I was chilled by the time I got back to the tent. I was shivering and found myself leaning closer to Theresa to try to get warm. By the third time I'd had to go to the bathroom, it was in the early morning hours, and all my shivering had woken Theresa. This time as I lay there shivering, she turned toward me and whispered, "Scoot over here."

I did as she said. Theresa wrapped her arms around me and pulled me close to her chest. I immediately felt warmer, partially because of her warmth and partly because of the rush of heat I felt from being in her arms with my head on the crook of her shoulder.

Her musky cologne smelled fantastic. Before I knew it, I was sound asleep again, and this time I didn't wake up until the next morning when Mom and Richard got up.

It was terrific sleeping snuggled up with Theresa. I was surprised by how I felt the immediate loss when she got up at the same time Mom and Richard did. It was more than her taking away her heat. It was losing the comfort of being in her arms too.

Chapter Twelve
Theresa

Dad and Mandy both were giving me a weird look when I got out of the tent, but it was Dad who asked, "What was that about?"

"I had to hold her down to keep her from getting up every few minutes," I grumbled. "It's a wonder I got any sleep."

"Ha, ha, funny," Patty said as she crawled out of the tent. "She got tired of me trying not to wake her when I kept moving closer and closer each time I came back from the bathroom freezing. So she wrapped me in a bear hug and tried to suffocate me."

Dad chuckled and shook his head, but Mandy was still giving Patty a questioning look.

"I was freezing, and she was helping me get warm. That's all," Patty said, and Mandy finally looked away.

Well, that kind of answered any questions I might have had about how Mandy would feel about how much I liked Patty. She apparently did not like the idea. Patty had surprised me this morning when she had easily slid into my arms and let me hold her, but she was freezing. She put her feet on my leg, and they were like ice cubes.

"Hopefully, the heater being on all night and day will help the mattresses dry out," Dad said.

"It's supposed to get up to almost seventy today. We might think about getting them out in the sun this afternoon," I suggested.

"That's a good idea," Dad agreed.

Patty had gone to her mom's car and was digging around in it. She pulled out their fishing poles. When she came back, she said, "I'm ready to get to the water. Who else is ready?"

"Let's do it," I said and got Dad's and my pole out from the back of the truck.

Mandy started the coffee while we were gathering our stuff. "Patty, please grab our mugs out of the bag in the backseat."

Patty did as she was told and came back to the camper. Dad had already got ours out. Mandy started filling the mugs and handing them out for us to doctor our own. I have to have enough sugar and creamer to cover the taste of the coffee. I mostly drink it for the caffeine. Patty only put sugar in hers, as did Mandy. Dad has always liked his black.

Mandy and Patty carried all the coffee mugs as Dad, and I hauled the chairs and poles down to the water's edge. I was a little worried about Patty coming down the slope, but it was a reasonably smooth and short walk. I could see that Mandy was watching Patty too.

It was six o'clock in the morning, and the sun was barely peeking over the horizon as we set up. It was still cold, so Dad and I built a small fire in the pit we'd put together at this spot. Patty stayed close to the fire. I don't think she'd gotten over the chill she had last night.

By eight o'clock, we'd caught two crappies and three bluegills. All of them big enough to make an excellent meal.

Mandy turned to Patty. "Let's go make some breakfast."

"Yeah, I need to go to the bathroom anyway," Patty agreed.

"You want me to come up and prep those for you?" Dad asked.

Mandy smiled sweetly. "No thank you, I've scaled and gutted enough fish in my day. And Patty needs the practice."

Patty was shaking her head and laughing at the same time. "Scaling is the only part I hate about fishing."

Tugging at Patty's arm, Mandy said, "Come on. I'm starving, and I expect Mattie is too."

Dad and I watched them go back up the hill. I put new bait on my hook and threw my line back out. After several minutes, Dad cleared his throat and asked, "So what really happened with you and Patty?"

I looked over at him. "She was really freezing. I could feel her trying to get close to me without touching me to try to get warm. The third time, I told her just to scoot over to me, and I wrapped my arms around her so I could help her get warm. That's it."

He nodded and went back to watching the water. After a little bit, he said, "You know I wouldn't care if something was going on with you two, but I'm not sure how Mandy will feel about it."

"There's nothing going on, Dad," I said. "I like her. She's nice, and we're becoming friends, but that's it. I don't think she plays for my team."

"Okay," he said. "I just wanted to tell you how I felt."

"Thanks," I said and then wondered if I was showing my crush on Patty more than I intended. I didn't think I was looking at her for too long or standing too close when we talked. I'd have to be more careful. I didn't want to make Mandy mad and lose this contract over a silly crush.

Later, when Patty and I were fishing by ourselves while Dad and Mandy tried to get the mattresses dry, Patty turned to me and asked, "Did your dad give you the third degree about this morning?"

"Yes," I said. "And to think we were worried about them. We didn't even do anything but try to keep you warm."

"I know," Patty said. "Who would have thought they would be so weird about it." She adjusted herself in her chair and rubbed her lower abdomen.

"Contraction?" I asked.

"Yeah, but just Braxton-Hicks," Patty winced. "I go to the doctor on Monday and then after that I'll go every week until she gets here."

"You are holding up really well," I said. "I'd probably be laid up in bed whining about the pain."

Patty laughed. "I doubt that. You're pretty tough. You only whined a little bit when you smacked your thumb with the hammer the other day."

"It only hurt for a little bit, not for nine months," I said.

"Well, I've had the Braxton-Hicks contractions for a few weeks. The worst part has been my back. It hurts a lot, but it'll be over soon and totally worth it," she said and tugged a little bit on her line.

"Well, I think you're very strong and brave," I said. "I can only imagine how much crap you've gotten at school over your condition."

Patty shrugged. "Just mostly from Caleb Dalton and his crew. Destiny and the cheerleaders."

"Destiny?" I asked.

"Caleb's girlfriend, Destiny Black," Patty said. "They've been dating since middle school. Caleb and I dated for a little while, but it was just a summer fling, which was all I intended it to be too. I wasn't in love with him. I was just drunk and high all the time, and he was paying for a lot of it."

"Really?" I asked, not really surprised, but sort of, "Wasn't he worried about getting drug tested for football?"

"Not if the coaches didn't find out, and Caleb didn't do anything to arouse their suspicions. Plus, those tests don't mean anything if you know how to flush your system, or use something that doesn't stay in the system long," Patty explained.

I didn't say anything for several minutes and then curiosity got the best of me. "So what was he buying for you?"

"Lots of stuff. Caleb had a friend who could get us alcohol, and another friend who sold pills," Patty said with a shrug. "It's amazing how easy stuff is to get if you know the right people and have money."

I nodded, knowing that was true.

"I definitely won't be doing any of that again. Not to say I might not have a beer or glass of wine occasionally, but I'll never let myself get so whacked out of control that I don't remember what I've done," Patty said quietly.

"Is the baby Caleb's?" I asked, and at first, I didn't think she was going to answer.

She stared out at the water. "I suppose it could be, but he always wore a condom. There were other guys around partying with us, and there were a few times that I truly don't remember what happened. I'd woke up on the couch at someone's house once and didn't know the people or how I got there. So, it's anyone's guess who the father is."

I reached over and put my hand on her arm. "I'm sorry I asked."

"No, it's the truth. Getting pregnant was the least of what could have happened," Patty said turning to look at me. "I was lucky. I didn't get any diseases that I won't be able to get rid of, and I didn't get killed."

Gently squeezing her arm, I said, "I'm glad none of those things happened. I wish I would have known you then. I might have been able to help you with what you were going through."

Patty patted my hand. "I don't think anyone could have helped me during that time and Caleb totally took advantage of my bad frame of mind. But, I believe in karma, and he'll get what's coming to him sooner or later. Now, let's talk about something happy, like what would it take to talk you into helping me set up Mattie's crib?"

"Share a pizza with me," I said.

"As long as I pay for it," she said.

"We'll see." I grinned.

Patty laughed and started reeling in her line. "I think we should go check to see what the lovebirds are up to. I hope they aren't drying the mattresses with their backsides."

I almost fell out of my chair laughing. "Yeah, I'll be sleeping in the tent again if that happened."

"Me too," Patty agreed.

Chapter Thirteen
Patty

"I can't believe you decided to sleep between Theresa and me last night," I said to Mom as we drove back to Riverton.

Mom just looked over at me.

"Seriously, do you honestly think we would have done something with you two in the bed next to us?"

Finally, Mom gave me a small smile. "I guess we were being a little silly."

"Ah, yeah," I agreed.

We didn't say much of anything else for several miles, and then I turned to her. "Would it really bother you that much if there was something between Theresa and me?"

Mom turned to me with mild alarm on her face. "Is there something you need to tell me?"

"No. I mean, I like her, but I don't think it's like that," I said.

"What do you mean you don't think it's like that?" Mom asked.

I rolled my eyes. "Never mind. But you kind of answered my question, and I think you're being very hypocritical."

"Whoa! Wait one minute," Mom demanded. "You say there's nothing going on between you, but then you ask how I would feel if there was. Is there something going on or not?"

"There's not," I said firmly and looked out the window. There wasn't, except that I felt cared for when I was around Theresa. And, I feel a little tingly when she touches me, but I decided I wasn't going to tell Mom that. I guess the possibility of me being gay on top of a druggy slut might be too much for her.

The rest of the ride was made in silence except for the radio playing on a light rock station. When we got back to Riverton, we went to the new house and unloaded the camping stuff and water there. Afterwards, we went to our apartment and went our separate ways. I took a shower and went to my bedroom to work on packing more of my stuff for the big move. Everything had to be out of the apartment by next Sunday night, so we would be making several trips to the house this week to move stuff into it. Theresa was finished with her part of the living room and the big bedroom so Mom and I would be painting tomorrow night. Mom talked about taking Tuesday off to paint, and I was planning on skipping school to help her.

I have thirty-five days of school left and could care less about missing a day. I was passing all my classes with As and Bs, so there was no fear of not graduating. Plus, it would be one more day I wouldn't have to worry about seeing Caleb or Destiny.

Daria sent me a text asking how the camping trip went. I texted her back and told her it was okay. I would have called her, but I figured she was busy with Robbie. If I were brave enough to admit it, I'd want to talk to Daria about how good it felt to be held by Theresa, but I still wasn't ready to acknowledge how much I enjoyed it.

Mom came into my room about an hour after we got home. "Can we talk?" she asked.

"I guess," I said and sat down on my bed. Mattie put a foot in my rib, and I had to shift my weight so that I was leaning away from Mom.

"The little girl moving around in there?" Mom asked.

"Yeah, but I think she's turned downward for good now. Her feet are mostly in my ribs all the time," I said.

"She should be pretty close to getting settled into birthing position," Mom said. "It's only five weeks now."

"Believe me, I'm counting down the days," I said. "I'm so ready for her to be here."

Mom laughed and put her hand on my belly where Mattie was kicking me. After petting my stomach for a few minutes, Mom turned to me, completely serious. "I want to make it clear to you that I don't have a problem with Theresa's sexuality, and if you find yourself going that way, I'm going to be a little afraid for you, but I will be supportive."

"You'll be a little afraid of me liking Theresa, or that I might be gay?" I asked.

"I guess a little of both," Mom admitted. "I think Theresa is a nice girl, but she's been out for a while and knows how hard it can be in a small town like this. She's also been hurt pretty badly before, so she might not be ready to be in a relationship again."

"Mom," I said taking her hand. "I know about what happened to Theresa. I was at the same high school when it was happening. I know that I'm catching a lot of crap from people over being pregnant. If something happens between Theresa and me, I think I'll be okay. But, honestly, I don't know how I really feel about her, except I like her. I enjoy her company, but I don't know if I like her more than that."

Sighing, I went on, "It's weird. I've never been in love, or even really super attracted to anyone. The thing with Caleb was just the drugs and the booze. I have no idea how I ended up dating him, except that he was suddenly always around and he kind of just took me over. With Theresa, I feel safe when she's around, and I don't think she would be the one to start anything. If I started feeling that way about her, I'd be the one to have to initiate a relationship." I smiled at her. "So don't start worrying until there's something to worry about, okay."

"Wow, spoken like a mother," she said.

"Well, I've got to get in practice since I'm getting ready to be one," I said.

Mom wrapped her arms around me, hugged me, and kissed me on the side of the head. "I wish so much that your father was alive to see how much you've grown up. He would be so proud."

"I hope so," I said.

"He would, and so am I," Mom said and looked into my eyes. "I was terrified for you, but you've really gotten your shit together. I'm so glad that you did."

"Thanks, Mom, me too. Not that I might not do some stupid things still, but I'm definitely staying away from the drugs and alcohol." I rubbed my stomach. "Mattie's going to make sure of that. Aren't you, baby girl?" Her response was a sound kick so we could see an impression of her whole foot making Mom and me laugh.

"Is she hungry for some pizza?" Mom asked.

"Well, of course, when is she not hungry," I said.

"Good, I'm hungry too. I'm going to order a supreme. How about we pick it up and eat it at the new house?" Mom stood and walked toward the door.

"Sounds like a plan to me," I said. "Are we taking some stuff over?"

"Yep, come on. Let's load some boxes in the car while I call in the pizza."

Chapter Fourteen
Theresa

John, Jesus, and I were upstairs cleaning up when I heard the front door of the house open. I had to make myself not rush downstairs and ask Patty about how her doctor's visit went.

It had been two weeks since the camping trip, and even though Patty and I are just starting friends, I was getting very excited about her baby being born. I wondered if she would look like Patty with her auburn hair and green eyes.

Finally, we were ready to haul the bags of trash down to the dumpster, so I'd have an excuse to see Patty and ask her about the doctor.

When I got downstairs, Patty and Mandy were painting in the living room. I liked the soft yellow Mandy had chosen. It was going to make it very bright and cheerful in here. They both turned and looked at us when we went through. I waved and continued going outside. When I came back in the house, I asked, "So how'd the doctor visit go?"

"Good," Patty said. "The doctor said she's turned and her head's low, so it's definitely getting close."

"When is your due date?" I asked.

"May thirtieth," Patty answered and then rubbed her lower abdomen," but I'm not sure if she's going to hold off that long. I've been having a lot of strong contractions."

"What I'm worried about is that she's going to have her next Friday when your father and I go to Bowling Green to pick up the claw tub I bought," Mandy said. "It would just be my luck that I'll be almost three hours away and she'd go into labor."

"Well, from what everyone has said, you should still have time to get back if I do," Patty said.

"I'm more worried about nobody being here to take you," Mandy said.

"I can drive, Mother. Your car will be here," Patty said indignantly.

"Trust me, when you're in the throes of labor, you are not going to want to be driving," Mandy said.

I was enjoying watching the bantering between mother and daughter, but like Mandy, I was worried about Patty being alone.

"I'll be at school for the graduation practice, or I can call Daria," Patty said.

"I could hang out with you that day," I volunteered.

"Would you do that?" Mandy asked, relieved.

"I don't want you to have to take off work just to watch me and a bunch of my classmates practice how not to fall off the stage on the football field," Patty said.

"I don't mind," I said. "And if you do go into labor I can rush you to the hospital and call your mom because I'll be there."

"I like it. That's what we'll do," Mandy said.

Patty rolled her eyes. "All right, whatever."

"Good," I said, relieved that Patty would not be at the mercy of a bunch of seniors who were going to be goofing off and probably not paying any attention to their pregnant classmate.

Later, when Mandy came upstairs to check on our progress, which was moving along very nicely, she took me aside and told me she was worried about Caleb Dalton and his friends. The graduation practice would be the first time he would be near her since the incident at school. Mandy said that she was positive she had seen Caleb's truck in their neighborhood and was afraid he was stalking Patty.

"I don't think that boy's right in the head," Mandy said. "He's probably still using whatever drugs he was getting for Patty, and I don't know...I've just always thought there was something evil about him."

"He's always kind of been like that," I said. "When I was friends with his sister, she told me about some stuff he had done, like torturing pets and burning important stuff of hers. He's just always got by with stuff because of who his parents are."

"Not this time," Mandy said firmly. "I've warned his father, and he should know that I mean business. I will get Caleb's punk ass put in jail if he keeps messing with Patty, even if I have to go all the way to the Attorney General's office."

"I'm more than happy to watch over her while you're gone," I said.

"Thank you, Theresa," Mandy said. "I will feel a lot better knowing that you are with her."

Chapter Fifteen
Patty

My lower back is killing me. The Braxton Hicks contractions are getting stronger. I keep timing each contraction just in case, but my doctor had told me these were my body prepping for delivery. If these were the false labor pains, I was terrified of what the real ones were going to be like.

Theresa is working upstairs by herself. She sent her guys home earlier. I find it very comforting that she is here. I know if I were to go into labor she would rush me to the hospital. In fact, she'd already been down to check on me twice in the hour since I'd been home from school.

I think, too, she just wanted to talk to me. Our friendship was becoming stronger all the time. I enjoy her company. The weird butterflies she stirs whenever she is around make me nervous. I'd never thought I would ever be attracted to another woman, but there is something about Theresa. She is strong, beautiful, and so gentle that I find myself wanting to be near her more and more.

I started dozing on the couch as I mulled over my feelings about Theresa. The heating pad I was laying on was soothing my back pain, and the ibuprofen was kicking in too. Sleep was slowly claiming me when I heard someone beating on the front door.

"Shit," I hissed, totally pissed off that someone had just interrupted a much-needed nap.

I got up, went to the front door and opened it, thinking it was one of Theresa's guys, but it was Caleb Dalton standing on my front porch.

"What the hell are you doing here?" I demanded.

"So it's true. You have moved out of the section eight housing," Caleb said looking past me to the inside of the house. "It doesn't look like much of an improvement though. I mean, other than the house is bigger and it's in a better neighborhood."

"What do you want?" I snapped. "You know you are not supposed to be within thirty feet of me."

He waved me off. "Oh, that is just Principal Whipple's rule. It's not a restraining order."

"I don't care. I don't want you near me," I said crossing my arms over my chest.

"Now that's not what you said last summer. You said you always wanted to be with me," he purred and moved to try to touch my arm.

I moved away from him, further out onto the porch. "That was before I figured out that you were just using me as your party bitch," I growled.

He turned and moved toward me again. "Now, now," he said, smiling. "You were enjoying all that partying. You liked all the booze and pills I was getting for you. I spent a small fortune keeping you on drugs."

"Drugs you were using too, Caleb," I snapped. "I wonder what UK's recruiters would have to say if they knew how much Oxy you've been using."

"Oh, I quit all that after school started back up," he said casually. "I was just doing it for fun during the summer. I particularly liked Ectasy as you recall. So did you. Maybe after you pop out that kid, I can hook you up with some."

"No thanks," I said. "I won't be using drugs anymore. My daughter and I will be living a very healthy life."

I was making a circle on the porch slowly heading back to the door where I planned to slip into the house and shut and lock the door. As I was approaching the door with Caleb stalking me, Theresa stepped out onto the porch.

"Patty? You okay?" she asked, moving to my side.

Caleb stopped stalking me and straighten. The glare he gave Theresa was filled with surprise and then hatred. "What are you doing here?"

"Patty and I are friends," Theresa said and put her arm around my shoulders.

"That's right," I said and put my arm around her waist. I noted that she didn't mention that she was working on the house.

The look on Caleb's face when I put my arm around her told me that the hatred he had for her had nothing to do with competing construction companies. It was personal. There was a clear and vibrant animosity between the two of them. I could feel Theresa's body tightening as if she were preparing for a fight.

Caleb's glare turned to me. "If that is my kid, it is not going to be around no dyke," he spat.

I smiled sweetly. "But, Caleb this is not your child. Even if the blood tests, which I'm not having, said it was, you signed your rights away months ago. You have no say in who I have this baby around. And Theresa and I have become good friends, so I'm sure she will be around the baby a lot."

For a moment I thought Caleb was going to combust right before our eyes. His face turned blood red, and his eyes bulged. "NO!" he shouted and started to back away. "She will not be a part of that kid's life. You will have a blood test done. I want to know if it's mine because she is not going to be near it if it is."

"Caleb, you have no say in the matter," I said firmly. "You don't have any rights as far as this baby is concerned and you never will."

He was shaking his head and backing away. "This is not over," he said before turning and storming to his truck.

Theresa and I continued to stand there with our arms around each other as he drove away. When he was out of sight, I turned in her arms and lay my head on her shoulder. "Thank God you were here."

She wrapped her arms around me and held me tightly. "Yes, thank God."

I pulled back and looked up at her. "I need a glass of tea now. How about you?"

"That would be great," she agreed.

We went to the kitchen together. I got the glasses out of the cabinets that still had no doors, and Theresa took the pitcher of tea out of the refrigerator. After she'd poured our glasses and put the pitcher back in the refrigerator, I said, "Let's go sit down on the couch and you can tell me the story behind you and Caleb."

At first, I thought she was going to say no, but then she let out a heavy sigh and nodded. "Okay."

She followed me to the living room and sat down on the opposite end of the couch from me. Usually, she didn't sit so far away, but she seemed to need some space for what she was about to tell me.

Taking a deep breath, Theresa began, "Do you remember the big bout of craziness at school when it came out that I was gay?"

"Yes," I said and sipped my tea. "Caleb's sister outed you." This was part of why I thought it was weird that Caleb was so angry with Theresa when she should have been the one angry at him. His sister, Linda ruined Theresa's life.

"Well, she did that to throw everyone off of the fact that she was gay too," Theresa said. She looked me directly in the eyes. "Linda and I were lovers."

My mouth dropped open. Linda Dalton had been the epitome of everything a perfect girl should be. She was at the top of every list: highest grades, best dressed, most popular, teachers' favorite, head cheerleader, valedictorian of her class. The list went on and on. She led a church fundraiser for needy families with her mother every Christmas.

There was a rumor that Linda had initiated the sexual contact with Theresa when they had been caught, but no one had said anything about them being lovers. Many people believed Theresa had sexually assaulted Linda.

"Yeah, that is the reaction most people have," Theresa said and sipped her tea.

Reaching down, she untied her work boots and took them off. She turned on the couch and sat cross-legged facing me. I couldn't sit cross-legged, so I turned on the couch, adjusted my heating pad and stretched out on the couch with my feet almost touching Theresa's knees.

"It started the summer of our senior year. We both had gone to Murray for summer programs. I was there for basketball, and she was there for cheerleading. There were five of us from Riverton down there, and we all hung out. Of course, we'd all been kind of friends before because we were all athletes, but we all got pretty close the two weeks we were there for the programs.

"Linda and I had always gotten along pretty good despite the fact that our fathers were big competitors. She wasn't interested in her father's business. Her mother was all about charities and fundraisers, and Linda was involved with that. She loved that she got to rub elbows with the upper crust of our community." Theresa paused to sip her tea. "I'd always thought she was pretty and nice. After we came home from Murray, Linda started inviting me out to do stuff with her on a regular basis. One day we were sitting in her room listening to music, and she was modeling some new dresses she'd gotten. I was reading the lyrics from one of the CD cases when she came over and sat on my lap. She said I wasn't paying attention to her. I looked up and realized that she was sitting on my lap in her underwear. Our eyes locked and then she kissed me." Theresa shook her head and looked away. I could see her eyes glistening with tears. "That kiss explained so many things that I didn't understand about myself. It had done that for her too." She sighed again. "Things progressed between us and I couldn't have been happier until school started. There was no way she could let her parents find out about us." Looking up at me, she said, "I'm sure you knew about her dating Tommy Cowan."

"Everyone knew," I said quietly.

Theresa nodded. "Linda told me she had to go back to dating Tommy when school started so her parents wouldn't suspect anything. School started, she and Tommy were a big thing again, but she was seeing me on the side."

I touched her knee with my barefoot. "That must have been awful for you."

"It was hard," she admitted. "But I would have done anything she wanted. I'd fallen hopelessly in love with her."

"Oh, Theresa, I'm so sorry," I said. I could only imagine how painful it must have been for her to see the girl she loved hanging all over her boyfriend.

Theresa wiped a stray tear that had escaped her eye and shrugged. "It was what it was."

"So, I take it that the Dalton family found out about the two of you," I prompted, more than curious to know how it had all come out.

"Oh yes," Theresa said and rolled her tea glass between her palms before taking a sip. She looked up at me and pursed her lips as if deciding how much to tell me.

"Come on," I said. "You can tell me."

With yet another heavy sigh, she nodded, "Caleb walked in on us in Linda's room."

"He walked in on you guys making out?" I asked, my mind immediately picturing Theresa and Linda in an embrace.

"More than making out." Theresa blushed.

My eyes widened. "You were…"

"She was," Theresa supplied.

I saw the image Theresa was alluding to with a clarity that surprised me almost as much as the heat that rushed through my body. "She was going down on you?"

Theresa's face turned blood red as she nodded.

"And Caleb walked in," I said picturing it in my head. I could see Caleb watching for a few minutes, registering what was happening before freaking out.

"He ran downstairs and got Linda's father. We both got dressed and raced downstairs. I was going to get the hell out of there because there was no saying that it wasn't what he thought it was. Linda's father met us in the foyer. He grabbed me and physically threw me out of the house and down the stairs of their front porch," Theresa said.

"You broke your arm," I said. "I remember you coming to school in a cast and then it was all over school that you'd attacked Linda."

Theresa's blush turned to anger. "Yes. But, more than that happened. When I got home with my broken arm, my father went into a rage. He called the police and had them meet us at the Dalton's house. Eric Dalton told the police that he threw me out of his house because Caleb caught me attacking Linda. I was forced to tell the police, in front of my dad, what had really happened. Unfortunately, Linda did not corroborate my story. She told the same story her father did."

I leaned over and picked up my tea shaking my head. I sipped it as I listened to Theresa continue her story.

"The police said they wouldn't charge me because it was their word against mine, and of course, they didn't charge Eric Dalton with assaulting me. Dad took me to the hospital. I was worried Dad was going to go back to the Daltons and beat the shit out of Mr. Dalton and end up in jail. But, the worst part was when we got home and had to explain to my mom what had happened." Theresa's jaw flexed as she gritted her teeth. "She said I was sick and that she would make arrangements to get me to a psychologist."

Now, I had both feet pressed against her knees and was stroking them with my toes. Theresa reached down with one hand and petted my left foot.

"Dad was already in the wrong frame of mind, and he went off on Mom. He said, 'How dare you say she's sick! There's nothing wrong with her, she's just gay.'" Theresa laughed bitterly. "Mom's response was, 'Well, of course, there's something wrong with her if she's was gay,' and the battle lines were drawn. Jonah sided with Mom agreeing that I was sick."

"So that's when things started going wrong for your parents?" I asked.

"No, things hadn't been good for a while," Theresa said. "Mom accused Dad of having affairs all the time because he was hardly ever home. Dad was working all the time to avoid her, and because she was spending money faster than he could make it."

"What did your mom do for a job?" I asked.

"Spend Dad's money," Theresa said sarcastically.

I raised an eyebrow.

"And she worked as a secretary at the construction company," Theresa admitted. "She wasn't like your mom, who went out and worked on the jobs. God forbid she get a little dirt on her. But, she worked with my grandmother at the construction company office."

"What did your grandparents say about what happened?" I asked, wondering what my own family would do. Mom had already said she would be okay with it, but I wasn't sure about my grandparents, well my mom's parents. Dad's parents were both pretty laid back.

"Party lines again, Mom's parents sided with her, Dad's with dad," Theresa said. "Mom's parents had always been mad about Mom and Dad being together. I never really understood it. Dad was always good to Mom. He gave her whatever she wanted. Dad's parents always treated Mom well. But, after the divorce, it came out that Mom had been pregnant and that was why she and Dad got married in the first place. Dad was doing the right thing."

"Sounds like your Dad got screwed all the way around," I said.

Theresa laughed. "Yeah, and stuck with me as part of the deal."

"I don't think he sees it that he got stuck with you," I said. "I think he sees you as the best thing to come of his marriage to your mother."

She rubbed my foot and ankle. "Thank you."

"So, back to the story. I'm guessing Linda and Caleb went to school and told everyone that you attacked Linda to cover for you having a broken arm and you and Linda no longer being friends," I said.

"Yep, that's exactly what happened, except Linda was having a hard time with the story. She knew it was wrong." Theresa teared up a little again. "And she loved me more than she wanted to admit." She wiped at the tears. "I'm not sure what happened. No one has ever told, but I think her parents forced her to go to therapy and she wasn't dealing well with all that was happening. When we came back from Christmas break, Linda wasn't at school. Even Tommy didn't know what had happened to her and Caleb wasn't talking to anyone. Caleb mean mugged me every time he saw me. I knew he blamed me for whatever had happened to Linda."

"Yeah, that was pretty clear out on the porch," I said.

Theresa smiled with raised eyebrows. "You think?" She turned serious. "Be careful around him; I don't think his head is completely screwed on right. Linda told me some stories about how mean he could be. He'd hurt her several times, and no one knew about it. She was afraid of him and her father."

"I could see her father being an abusive man," I said. "Her mom always struck me as a stuck up bitch, but I could see her taking a few punches and keeping her mouth shut in order to keep being Eric Dalton's wife. I've heard he's planning on running for a state legislature position next election."

"Great. I really want to see his self-righteous mug on the news every other night," Theresa said bitterly.

Mom came in the front door just then. She looked from me to Theresa. "You guys look like you're getting a lot of work done," she said and set her purse down on the overstuffed chair just inside the door.

Theresa patted my foot one more time and said, "That's my cue to get back at it."

"I was just teasing," Mom said.

"I've been on break for a good bit though," Theresa said looking at her watch and then at me. "Almost an hour, but I appreciate the talk."

"I'm glad we talked," I said sitting up. "And thank you for coming to my rescue with Caleb."

Mom had just come over to rub my stomach, something she loved doing. "As in Caleb Dalton? Oh look, she's moving her foot along your stomach."

Theresa and I both looked at the little bump that traveled across the top of my belly.

"Wow, that is amazing," Theresa said.

"You want to feel it?" Mom asked.

Theresa's mouth opened in surprise, and she looked at me.

"Go ahead. It's really neat to feel her moving."

Putting one of her long hands on my belly right where Mattie had been putting her foot, Theresa's face lit up with delight as Mattie rewarded her effort by running her foot along the same route. "That is so cool," Theresa said.

"Yeah, feeling her move around is my favorite part of being pregnant," I said. "But, I'm ready for her to come out too."

Theresa asked. "When are you guys having your baby shower?"

"After graduation," Mom said. "That's when her Dad's parents can come. They moved to Florida after Pat passed away, so we don't see them much."

"That's wonderful," Theresa said.

"You're going to come, of course," Mom said. "You and your father both."

"We wouldn't miss it for the world," Theresa said.

"Now, what was Caleb Dalton doing here?" Mom demanded.

"He was here to harass me," I said. "Fortunately, Theresa came out onto the porch. He started flipping out, saying that if the baby was his, he didn't want it to be around a dyke. His word. I told him this was not his child regardless of what any blood test said. He signed away his rights months ago."

"That's right," Mom said, standing. "I'm going to call the police and tell them he was here. How does he even know where we live now?"

"I don't know," I said and swung my feet off the couch as Theresa stood.

"I'm going to head back upstairs and get a few more hours in," Theresa said. "It should be ready to paint tomorrow, the next day at the latest and then we'll work on the yard and gardens for a few days while the weather is good."

"Thank you, Theresa," Mom said. "For all the great work you guys are doing, and for being here for Patty today."

"I was glad I was here too," Theresa said and looked at me. "Anytime you need my help, don't hesitate to call me, okay?"

"I will, I promise," I said.

Mom and I watched her go up the stairs. "She's a sweet girl," Mom said.

"Yes, she is," I agreed and then whispered. "She told me about what happened with the Daltons after Caleb left."

"Really?" Mom sat down on the couch next to me. "Her father said she never talks about it."

I leaned closer to mom and said in a low tone, "I think it helped her telling me about it. It made me hurt for her. I wonder if she's ever trusted another woman."

"Not according to Richard," Mom said softly. "He said she's never mentioned being involved with anyone, and he knows all she does now is work."

I looked toward the top of the stairs. "That's sad. She's so pretty and nice."

Mom raised an eyebrow at my comment, making me wonder if I'd said too much, but she just nodded and agreed, "Yes, she is."

Chapter Sixteen
Theresa

I've become more vigilant since Caleb showed up at Mandy and Patty's house. Based on what Linda told me, Caleb is a sick freak, and I am terrified he is going to try to hurt Patty. I told Mandy that I didn't think Patty should be alone at all since she's so close to her due date. Mandy agreed. We'd made a pact that if for some reason Mandy couldn't take Patty to school, or pick her up that I would do it.

Now that Patty and I had both spilled our guts to each other about our past transgressions, we'd become very close. Patty would come out to the yard after school to help with planting the new flower beds. I tried to stop her, but she said it wouldn't hurt her to sit on the grass and bury bulbs in the gardens. I'd work alongside her, and we talked about everything.

Patty is bright and it's fun talking to her. She knows a lot about art and history. We talked about how our families have lived in this area for a very long time and have ties to the Native American history that has been preserved in several places nearby. We've talked about taking the baby to powwows and art festivals.

I find that I feel happy just seeing her standing around watching us work when she doesn't feel like helping. How strong my feelings are becoming scares me. I'd hate to mess up my friendship with Patty, and

I would hate to cause problems for Dad and Mandy, who seem to be getting closer to having a relationship.

My phone started buzzing in my pocket, and I had to wait until Jesus finished nailing the crown trim we were putting up in the upstairs bedrooms before I could check the message left when I didn't answer.

The message was from Mandy asking if I could pick up Patty today. I called her back and assured her that I could get Patty, which meant that I would have to leave right away. "Hey, I've got to run over to the high school and pick up Patty," I told Jesus and John.

"No, problem," John said. "We'll finish this room while you're gone."

"You guys want me to pick up some tea from McDonald's on my way back?" I asked as I took off my tool belt.

"Yes!" they both said.

Waving, I turned and bound down the stairs and out to my truck. I was excited about getting Patty. We hadn't had much time to talk last night because I was exhausted. It had been a gorgeous day yesterday, so we spent the day working on the yard at Mandy's and on a new job I'd contracted that was just redoing the gardens. It had been late when I got home, but I called Patty anyway, mostly just to hear her voice.

When I got to the high school, I went to the student parking lot. I'd texted Patty before I left the house to let her know where I'd pick her up. I parked in a handicap spot, which I know is wrong, but considering Patty's delicate condition, she didn't need to walk all the way to the back of the parking lot.

There were only ten school days left, according to Patty and fifteen days until Mattie was due to arrive. I could tell things were getting hard for Patty. She grimaced a lot and complained about how much her back was hurting.

When I saw her coming out of the school, I got out of my truck and went around to the passenger side to open the door for her. She was trying to walk fast, but her size was slowing her down. There were a group of girls following behind her. I couldn't hear what they were saying, but I could tell that Patty was trying to get away from them. Walking toward Patty, I felt my protective side preparing for a fight.

When Patty was a few steps from me, she whispered, "I'm going to kiss you." She said it so quietly I wasn't sure I'd heard correctly.

The girl who appeared to be the leader of the pack following Patty looked me up and down and said, "Well, it looks like you've gone from slut to dyke, Patty."

Patty looked up at me, it was clear she was trying to contain her anger, and then she turned to the girl and smiled. "That's right, Destiny. I've decided I prefer being with a woman who knows how to use her tongue for something more than telling lies."

Patty turned back to me, leaned in and kissed me. It was not just a peck on the lips, but a deep, thorough kiss. I almost lost my balance when her tongue touched mine, so I put my hands around her waist to steady myself.

When Patty stepped back, she looked surprised for a moment, but then turned to face Destiny. The whole group was staring with their mouths hanging open in shock. Behind them, I could see Caleb Dalton. His fists were clenched at his sides as he started to walk forward but stopped when Principal Whipple approached the group.

"What's going on?" Principal Whipple demanded.

Destiny recovered from her shock quickly and answered, "Nothing, Principal Whipple. We are just headed to our cars."

Principal Whipple apparently wasn't buying that. He looked over the group and asked Patty, "Everything okay, Ms. McNeal?"

"Yes, sir. Theresa came over to help me into her truck," Patty said and put her hand on her huge belly to emphasize her point.

Nodding, Principal Whipple said, "Yes, you need to be very careful." He turned and looked in the direction Caleb had been standing moments earlier. Caleb was gone. Destiny and her crew quickly dispersed toward their cars. Principal Whipple turned toward parking lot. Shaking his head, he looked at me and smiled. "It's good to see you, Theresa."

"Good to see you too, sir," I said.

"I hear you're working for your father and doing a wonderful job," Principal Whipple said, turning his full attention to me. "My wife's friend, Esther Doan said you did a fabulous job with her garden. We might be interested in having you look at ours."

I pulled my wallet out of my back pocket and took out a business card. Handing it to him, I said, "Give me a call, and I'll come by and take a look at it."

"We'll do that," he said and put the card in his front shirt pocket.

"I need to get home and lay down," Patty said, pulling on my arm.

"Have a good evening," I said to Principal Whipple and then put my arm around Patty and led her to my truck. I helped her up into the seat and went around to the driver's side and got in.

"Thank you for coming to get me," Patty said leaning her head back against the headrest and closing her eyes. "It's been a long day."

"Getting ready for finals?" I asked as I joined the long line of cars leaving the parking lot.

"Yeah and dealing with assholes," Patty said but didn't open her eyes.

"That girl and her friends been giving you a hard time today?" I asked.

"Yeah, I guess she's trying to get a bunch of insults end before the end of the school year," Patty said and turned to me. "Sorry for attacking you like that. I just wanted to shut her up."

I smiled. "It was quite alright. You're a pretty good kisser, and you did exactly what you set out to do. All of them looked very surprised."

Patty smiled, laid her head back on the headrest and closed her eyes again. "You're a good kisser too."

Chapter Seventeen
Patty

It's the last Saturday before the last week of school. Finals are Monday and Tuesday, and Wednesday is the last day of school, which of course, I have no intention of attending. Thursday we have a graduation practice, so everyone knows where they are supposed to be. Saturday afternoon is graduation, and then it's all over. Thank God!

I can hear Theresa and her crew outside working in the yard. Theresa told me last night that they were going to work in the yard today because it was going to be such a lovely day. They are really close to being done with the outside gardens. Well, at least as done as they could be until things start blooming.

Everything was coming together very nicely. I'd slept in until almost ten. The Braxton-Hicks had me up most of the night. There was once I thought we were going to have to go to the hospital, but then Mattie settled down, and I was finally able to go to sleep.

When I got up, I could hear Theresa and the guys outside. I fixed breakfast and then sat down in the living room with my homework. Close to noon, I went out to check on the progress Theresa had made, plus I wanted to see her.

We hadn't talked about the kiss at school the other day, but I hadn't been able to stop thinking about it. The surge of electricity that I'd felt when we kissed was unlike anything I'd ever experienced. I knew she had felt it too by the surprised look on her face. Still, neither of us had mentioned it. I guess we're both afraid of what it might mean.

"Hey," Theresa said when I walked to the edge of the flower bed they were planting.

"How're things coming?"

Theresa stood from her bent over position and rubbed her lower back. "We will be done today. After that, it will be up to you and your mom to keep it weeded."

"What?" I asked in mock surprise. "You're not going to come over and pull every little weed out of the gardens?"

"Oh no," Theresa said with a grin.

"Are you guys going to break for lunch soon?" I asked.

"Not until closer to one," Theresa said. "We'll be done with this side of the yard by then. After lunch, we're going to wrap up the other side of the yard."

"Okay," I said, a little disappointed because I'd hoped to get to talk with Theresa now. "How about I make you all some ice tea?"

"That would be great," Jesus said wiping his brow.

Theresa grinned at me. "Yes, that would be great."

"Okay, I'm going to fix some. I'll bring it out in a few minutes," I said and headed back into the house.

I started tea for Theresa and her guys and then went into the living room. "Lord, being pregnant sucks," I moaned as I sank down on the couch.

"I bet."

I jumped and screamed when I heard Caleb's voice come from the doorway of the parlor.

"What the hell are you doing here?" I demanded.

"I came to see my baby momma," he sneered.

"This baby isn't yours," I snapped. "Regardless of what the blood tests say."

"Don't be so sure about that," Caleb said and took a menacing step toward me. "Just because my father made me sign those papers doesn't mean that I'm not going to claim the child. In fact, I might even insist we get married."

"When hell freezes over," I said and scooted farther away from him.

"Oh now, come on, Patty," Caleb cooed and moved closer. "We had a lot of fun last summer. I've got some really sweet X that will have you crawling all over me."

"Have you lost your mind?" I said, "I'm nine months pregnant. I'm not doing Ecstasy with you. I wouldn't even if I wasn't pregnant. I'm done with all that shit."

"We'll see," Caleb growled and rushed at me.

I jumped up planning to try to run for the back door, but he grabbed me and threw me down on the couch. "Get off me asshole!" I screamed, and I tried to get my knee in his groin, but his leg blocked the move and then he took both my hands in one of his big paws.

He held my hands above my head and tried to force my legs apart. I was crying and trying to fight him as hard as I could, but I was also trying to protect my stomach. Finally, he shoved a knee hard between my legs and put his full body weight on me. I was frantically trying to think of something I could do to fight him off, bite him, or something when I saw Theresa behind Caleb, pulling him off me.

The look on her face was pure rage. I hadn't seen her be more than mildly angry before. Today, she had a look on her face that I hope I never see again. The anger, disbelief, and fear were all wrapped up in a white-hot emotion that radiated from her. She looked beautiful and terrifying all at the same time.

When Caleb stood and faced her, I did not doubt that Theresa would come out the winner if Caleb tried to fight her, but if she didn't, she had John and Jesus backing her I noted when I saw the two men racing in the front door.

Chapter Eighteen
Theresa

Patty hadn't been back in the house to make the tea, but a few minutes when I would have sworn I heard her scream. I walked to the edge of the porch and saw Caleb Dalton's truck parked in front of the house. "John and Jesus come on!" I yelled urgently and jumped onto the porch.

I burst into the house with John and Jesus on my heels. Caleb had Patty down on the couch. He had one knee between her legs, one hand holding both of hers over her head, and the other was trying to pull her pants down. I saw the panicked look on Patty's face and lost any sense of control that I might have had when I entered the room. I grabbed Caleb by his shirt and pulled him off of Patty.

He jumped to his feet and turned to face me, raising his fist as he did. He stopped before he swung when he saw John and Jesus standing behind me.

"Brought your Spic crew to help you, bitch?" Caleb sneered.

"You need to watch your mouth asshole," Jesus said in his extreme southern voice.

That surprised Caleb momentarily. "You still look like a Spic," Caleb said.

John and Jesus were both very proud of their Hispanic heritage. John came up beside me. "Yeah, and this Hispanic is going to kick your nasty white ass."

"That's right because you're not man enough to fight me," Caleb said to me and spat in my face.

Years of simmering anger rushed to the surface, and I punched Caleb in the face so fast and hard that he didn't have time to react.

He grabbed his face and howled in anger. I knew I'd most likely broke his nose, but I didn't care. I grabbed him by his hair and shoved him toward the door. "Open the door!" I ordered John and Jesus.

They both went to the door and opened it wide. Caleb went to swing at me, I dodged his fist and put my work boot in his crotch. He bent over grabbing himself. I turned him toward the door, put my foot on his butt and pushed him toward the door, sending him sprawling onto the porch. Going out to stand next to him, I said, "You better get your ass up and get out of here."

"Fuck you," Caleb snapped and started to get to his feet.

I could hear sirens coming, and I knew Patty had called the police. I stepped back and waited to see what Caleb would do. When he heard the sirens, he jumped up as quickly as he could with his bleeding nose and sore testicles. "This is not over," he hissed as he went to his truck.

"You better hope it is," I shouted at him as he got in his truck. He started the engine and raced away before the police arrived.

I went back into the house and sat down next to Patty, who threw herself into my arms. This was the second time she'd needed me to hold her after an incident with Caleb. It felt good to be able to provide her comfort. "It's going to be okay now," I assured her. "Did he hurt you?"

"Not much," she said and then groaned. She gripped my arms tightly.

"What's wrong?" I asked, worried that Caleb had somehow started her labor.

"Just a Braxton Hicks," she said and released me as the contraction passed.

"Tee," John called from the door. "The police are here."

I got up and went out onto the porch as an officer I recognized got out of his car. It was Bill Wilson, thank God. At least we got someone who wouldn't automatically judge the scene based on the fact that two Hispanic men were standing around a blood stain on the porch.

"Theresa," Bill said as he recognized me and then he looked at the blood on the porch. "What happened?"

"Caleb Dalton attacked Patty McNeal. Her mom owns this house," I said.

"She inside?" he asked.

"Yeah," I said and motioned my head toward the door where Patty had come out to the porch.

"Miss McNeal, you want to tell me what happened?" Bill asked.

Patty nodded. "I'd just got through starting some tea and was getting ready to come out and get Theresa, John, and Jesus. I'd told them I'd make them some tea," Patty said, clearly still shaken. "When I came into the living room, Caleb was here. He grabbed me and threw me down on the couch. He was trying to rape me when Theresa, John, and Jesus came into the house and pulled him off me. I'm not sure what happened next."

"Caleb swung on Theresa, and she punched him in the face," John said.

Jesus added, "And when he came at her again she kicked him in the nuts."

Bill pulled out his notepad and started taking notes. He went back out to the porch. "Is this Mr. Dalton's blood?"

"Yes, sir," I said. "He fell on his face when I gave him a push outside."

"Where is he now?" Bill asked.

"He took off when he heard the sirens. Patty and her mom have already had harassment charges pressed at school," I said. "I'm not sure if the school's police officer filed an official report."

"We couldn't file a restraining order because he hadn't physically threatened me and we weren't in a relationship," Patty said, moving closer to me and taking hold of my arm for support. I patted her hand as I looked down into her tear stained face.

"Well, you'll be able to file one now," Bill said. He took out a small camera and took several pictures of the porch and blood stains. He pointed toward the house. "You said he assaulted you in the living room?"

"Yes," Patty confirmed. "He grabbed me and threw me on the couch."

Bill went into the house, and we followed him. He took pictures of the living room and then squatted where there were drops of blood on the floor. He looked at me. "This where you punched him?"

"Yes," I said.

He took more pictures and said, "Don't clean any of this up until after I talk to Mr. Dalton."

"Yes, sir," Patty said.

Mandy burst through the front door. "Whose blood is on the porch?"

"Caleb Dalton's," I said.

"Caleb?" Mandy looked confused, and then angry. "He was here?"

"Yeah, he attacked Patty," I said.

Patty went to her mother, who wrapped her in her arms. "Are you okay, Baby?" Mandy asked.

Shaking her head no, Patty started crying, "Why won't he leave me alone?"

"I don't know, Baby," Mandy said. She looked at Bill. "I want to file charges."

"Yes, ma'am," Bill said. He took out his notebook and made more notes. He spoke into the radio on his shoulder, asking someone to come out to the house. "I'm going to have a unit go out to the Dalton's place and pick up Caleb. I'm going to have another officer stop by and take another round of statements, just to make sure everyone is telling the same story. Mayor Dalton is going to demand we have serious proof that Caleb attacked Miss McNeal."

Another patrol car pulled up, and two officers got out. Bill had them take John and Jesus' statements, while he did the official forms for Patty and me. When we were almost done, Bill got a call on his radio. I don't know much about police code, but I gathered that they had not found Caleb.

Bill confirmed that when he said, "Mr. Dalton is not at his home or his father's business. I'm going to suggest that you guys stay inside tonight and keep the doors locked. If he shows up here, call 911. Do not talk to him, just call us and we'll come right back out." He turned to me. "Based on the witnesses' testimony, you were defending yourself, so I won't be charging you with assault, but I don't want you to have any more contact with Mr. Dalton."

"Trust me; I will be avoiding him unless he shows back up here while I'm still here. I won't confront him, but I will defend myself, Patty, and Mandy if necessary."

"Fair enough," Bill said and turned to Mandy. "There will be extra patrols around your house tonight. We'll let you know when we find him."

"Thanks, Officer Wilson," Mandy said.

I walked outside with Bill. He turned to me as we approached the edge of the yard. "I know about your history with the Daltons."

"I know you do," I said. Bill's daughter, Wendy was one of my best friends in high school.

"I want you to try not to have any more confrontations with him. His father is going to have a fit about all this." When I started to protest, Bill held up his hand. "I know Caleb started it, but you know how it works. His dad is the mayor, and he has many lawyers on speed dial. You have three witnesses that have testified that you were defending yourself, but you know Dalton is going to try to put a spin on anything else that happens. Do not go near him if you're alone, not that I don't think you can defend yourself." He assured me. "I just don't want to have to arrest you for something you didn't do."

"I promise. I'll be here or at home. I have a contract with Mandy, and I've got at least two more weeks of work here. I won't even go to the store other than to get gas."

Bill nodded. "Wendy told me to tell you hello if I saw you around."

I smiled. "She doing okay?"

"Yep, she'll be home this summer. You and your dad should come out sometime," he said.

"We'll do that," I promised.

Bill got in his car and drove off. I went back to the porch where Mandy, Patty, John, and Jesus stood talking. "You want us to get back at it?" John asked.

"Nah, let's call it a day," I said. "I think we could all use a rest."

"And a beer," Jesus said.

"Amen," John agreed and then turned to me. "Meet you here at eight tomorrow?"

"Nah, tomorrow is Sunday. Let's meet back here Monday at eight."

"Sounds good," John said. He and Jesus turned and went around the side of the house to gather all the tools while I stayed on the porch with Mandy and Patty.

"How are you?" I asked Patty.

"I'm okay. Just shaken up," Patty said and rubbed her stomach. "Mattie didn't like all that excitement, and she's letting me know about it."

"I don't blame her," Mandy said. "I didn't like all that excitement either."

Mandy turned to me. "Thank you for coming to Patty's rescue."

"I'm happy we were here. I hate to think of what would have happened if we weren't," I said, starting to feel shaky myself as the realization of what could have happened set in.

"We're not going to take any more chances," Mandy said. "I want to make sure someone is with Patty all the time now. She's too close to giving birth and I don't think Caleb is done unless they put his ass in jail."

"Which is not going to happen, and even if they did, his father would have him out in less than twenty-four hours," I said.

"Exactly," Mandy agreed.

"Well, anytime you need me to help out, you just let me know. And I know Dad will help too," I said.

"Thank you, Theresa. I may have to take you up on that," Mandy said.

"Please don't hesitate," I said looking into both of their beautiful green eyes. "I'm here for both of you." And I meant that with all of my heart.

Chapter Nineteen
Patty

I feel like I'm watching over my shoulder all the time now. Theresa was right about Caleb, he was out of jail in less than twenty-four hours after he was arrested.

Eric Dalton was trying to have charges filed against Theresa for punching Caleb in the face, but Theresa said the police weren't going to let him.

We filed assault and trespassing charges against Caleb. This time the judge gave us a restraining order. The only time Caleb can be within a thousand feet of me is when we are at school. As a result of the restraining order, Principal Whipple had me escorted from classroom to classroom by a teacher Monday and Tuesday. Wednesday I didn't bother to go to school because it was the last day and I had already said my goodbyes to everyone I cared about on Tuesday.

Even though I didn't see Caleb looking at me those last two days of school, I felt like I was being watched by one of his friends.

Destiny stared daggers at me every time I saw her. On Tuesday morning, she had a note passed to me that accused me of ruining her life by getting Caleb put in jail. I wrote her back and told her that he tried to rape me and that I had witnesses. I didn't see her again after that.

We are going to have our graduation practice on the football field in a half an hour, where the ceremony is supposed to take place as long as it doesn't rain. If it rains, we'll have it in the gym. We had the gym practice already. Officer Craig and a few other police officers were on hand to watch over us. Honestly, it didn't make me feel any safer. If Caleb is really nuts and decides to bring a gun to the practice, there won't be much Officer Craig could do.

When Principal Whipple and the teachers who will be helping with the graduation led us out of the school to the fields, Daria came up to me with Robbie in tow. "So, are you going to make it to graduation before you pop?"

I smiled and rubbed my huge stomach. "I hope so. It would just be my luck she'll decide to come on graduation day."

"I hope she waits until right after everyone gets their diplomas, then we can have a big baby drama and make graduation even more memorable," Daria said.

Laughing, I said, "Yeah, that would make it memorable alright."

I saw Theresa standing by her truck next to the ball fields. She was picking me up today because Mom and Richard were picking up the claw bathtub for the guest bathroom. They were supposed to get it a couple of weeks ago, but they guy Mom bought it from was out of the state. He was back in Bowling Green for a few days so they had to get it today. Mom was glad to go ahead and go because I would be at school part of the day. For some reason, she seemed to think that would keep me from going into labor.

I was a little worried that I might have the baby before graduation this weekend. Mattie hadn't been moving a lot, and I had a lot of pressure pushing down on my pelvis. At my last doctor visit three days ago, the doctor said I was dilated to one, but I could stay that way for a few weeks.

Principal Whipple saw Theresa standing by her truck and went over to talk to her. They spoke for a few minutes and then Principal Whipple looked in my direction and nodded.

We continued to make our way to the football field, and then Coach Bentley started having us lineup in order by our last names. Caleb turned and glared at me as he got in line. Coach Bentley moved into his line of sight and said something curt to him.

Daria and Robbie moved to the back of the line. There were roughly a hundred and fifty seniors, so it was a pretty long line. The chairs were already placed, and we marched onto the field and then in and out of the rows until we reached our seats. Principal Whipple, the vice principal, Mr. Gordon, and the guidance counselor, Mrs. Petty stood on the stage. Coach Bentley, Mrs. Jones, Mrs. Miller, Mr. Wilson and Mr. Goad chaperoned us to our seats.

Principal Whipple went over the basics of the ceremony as he had in the gym. They explained how each row would rise and make their way to the stage that had been built on the football field. Our parents, friends, and families would sit in the bleachers surrounding us. The band would play, and it would be beautiful, in theory.

It was gorgeous today, a little warm, but perfect weather. I wish we were having the graduation now and then it would be over. Just a few more days I told myself, and then I could focus on getting ready for Mattie's arrival.

When we finished the graduation practice everyone started back to the school to get their stuff, which we were not allowed to bring out with us. I waved at Theresa as we headed toward the school and she waved back. I wasn't really watching where I was going, but I should have been okay. There was a slight ravine that we had to cross to get to the parking lot. It wasn't more than four feet high, but the grass was a little slippery. I turned to look at Daria, who was calling out my name, and then I saw Caleb rushing at me. I froze, and he slammed into me, pushing me backward onto my butt and lower back.

"Patty!" I heard several people yell as I cried out in pain and felt a flood of fluid gush out between my legs.

The next thing I knew, Theresa was sliding down the hill next to me. "Are you okay?"

"No!" I cried. "I think my water just broke. God, I hope I didn't hurt the baby." I started crying.

Theresa wrapped her arms around me and looked at Daria, who had just knelt at my side. "Her water broke. We should call 911."

Mrs. Miller already had her phone to her ear calling the paramedics.

Mrs. Jones and Principal Whipple rushed over, "Is she okay?" They asked simultaneously.

"Her water broke," Daria informed them.

I could hear yelling and a big commotion in the general direction of the parking lot. Principal Whipple stood and started running in the direction of the noise.

"It's going to be okay," Theresa said, holding me against her chest.

"You're going with me to the hospital, right?"

"Of course," Theresa assured me.

"Have you called her mom?" Daria asked Theresa.

"No," Theresa said. "My phone is in the truck charging."

"I'll call," Daria offered.

I could see her looking from me to Theresa. I didn't care what she thought might be going on between us, which still wasn't anything, except that I needed her right now and she was here.

It seemed like forever before the ambulance finally arrived. Principal Whipple came back and informed us that several of the football players had helped Officer Craig wrestle Caleb to the ground and he was on his way back to jail.

The sad thing about living in a small town is that you know everyone and they know you, so when the ambulance arrived, the two techs were guys who had been friends with my parents for years. Thankfully there was also a woman, who I didn't know. I knew she would be the one who would most likely check me to see what was going on with the baby.

They pushed everyone back away from me, but I held on to Theresa, so she didn't move. I knew they would be taking me to Paducah and it was going to be a very long ride, even though it was only thirty minutes away.

When they put me on the stretcher and started wheeling me toward the ambulance, I said, "Theresa has to come with me."

The techs looked at Theresa, who said, "I'm the closest family. Her mother's on her way back from Bowling Green."

The guys who knew me, probably knew that wasn't true, but I was adamant.

"She has to come with us," I cried. "She's the father!"

The woman tech said, "Alright."

Theresa turned to Daria. "Will you call her mom and tell her I went with Patty to the hospital?"

"Yep, and we'll be right behind the ambulance," Daria promised.

As I suspected, the ride was long and crazy. The ambulance was flying, and Theresa looked scared.

"She's not going to have the baby before we get to the hospital, is she?" Theresa asked.

"Probably not," the woman tech said. "But she has dilated to three, and her blood pressure is a little high." She turned to me and said, "I want you to breathe through the contractions, not hold your breath. Did you take Lamaze classes?"

"Yes," I hissed as a powerful contraction took hold of me.

She turned to Theresa and asked, "Did you go with her?"

"No, her mother did," Theresa answered.

"Well, it's important for her to breathe through the contractions. I want you to help her do that, okay?"

"Okay," Theresa said. She had her hand on my shoulder, and I reached out and took her other hand. Smiling she said, "Let me know when one's coming, and we'll breathe through it, okay."

I nodded.

We breathed through several contractions until we arrived at the hospital, where there was a crazy rush of activity. I was taken out of the ambulance and whisked to a birthing room that was already set up.

The hospital had gotten word to my doctor, who was on call, thank God. Theresa was standing at the back of the birthing room watching everything that was going on with a look of mild horror. A nurse finally noticed her and growled, "Who are you? If you're not family, you can't be in here."

Theresa opened her mouth and looked at me. I shouted at the nurse. "She's the father. She stays."

The nurse turned back to Theresa, who shrugged and smiled weakly. The nurse snorted and then said, 'Well, then get over there on the other side of the bed, but stay out of the way."

Theresa hurried over to the head of the bed next to me. I took her hand and squeezed it tightly. She looked down at me and smiled reassuringly. "It's going to be okay."

"I know," I said weakly and then gripped her hand hard as a contraction slammed through me.

Dr. Denton came into the room and looked at me. "I thought you wanted to wait until after graduation?"

"Apparently Mattie is ready now," I hissed as I tried to breathe through the contraction.

Smiling, Dr. Denton put on her gloves and said, "Well, let's just see how ready she is."

Chapter Twenty
Theresa

"Yep, we're going to have a baby tonight," the doctor said confidently.

I looked down at Patty whose face was red and sweaty as she finally released my hand after I'm assuming the contraction had passed.

"You're at five now, and very thin, so we're going to start getting ready," the doctor informed her. "Do you still want an epidural?"

"Yes," Patty said firmly.

"Okay, I'll get Dr. Benote down here to talk to you about that. I heard you had a nasty fall earlier?"

"Yes," Patty said through gritted teeth.

The doctor nodded. "Mattie's vitals look good, but we'll get a portable ultrasound machine up here and take a quick look to make sure the umbilical cord is not near her neck, but I think she's going to be fine. Are you hurt anywhere because of the fall?"

"My lower back and butt," Patty said. "The lady in the ambulance said it looked like it might be bruised."

"Go ahead and take your feet out of the stirrups and scoot up on the bed. I want to take a look," Dr. Denton said as she took off her gloves. "Roll toward..." She looked up at me.

"Theresa," I supplied and helped Patty roll toward me. The doctor moved the wires they hooked to Patty's stomach and lifted her gown to

Page 137

reveal her lower back and butt. She pushed in a few places, and Patty winced. "Yeah, you definitely bruised this area, possibly your tailbone." She frowned. "That might make getting an epidural extremely painful. I'll talk to Dr. Benote about it."

"You mean I might not be able to have one?" Patty asked, looking over her shoulder at the doctor.

"It just might be very painful," the doctor said and then asked as she rolled Patty over to her back, "Is your mom on her way?"

"Yes. She was in Bowling Green picking up a tub for our new house." She nodded in my direction. "Theresa was watching over me today."

Dr. Denton looked in my direction and smiled. "It's nice to meet you, Theresa. And you are a cousin? Friend?"

The nurse who had told me I couldn't be in here unless I were family turned to look at me. Before I could answer, Patty reached out and retook my hand. "She's my girlfriend."

The doctor didn't bat an eye, but the nurse turned away. "Well, that's wonderful," the doctor said and patted Patty's knee. "I've got a few other people to check on. I'll be back when they get the ultrasound machine in here." She turned to the woman who seemed to be the main nurse. "Call me if you need me."

The nurse nodded and then went about putting some information in the computer. "In the rush earlier, I didn't get to introduce myself," the nurse said. "I'm Elizabeth. I'm going to be your nurse for the evening." She turned and pointed to the nurse who clearly didn't like the fact that Patty said I was her girlfriend. "This is Reina. She'll also be helping with your delivery. In a little while, the pediatric nursing team will come in and make sure everything is ready for the baby. Do you already have a pediatrician?"

"Yes. Grace Peterson is going to be Mattie's doctor," Patty said.

"Okay. Dr. Peterson is not a pediatrician at this hospital, so the doctor on call will be here to check out the baby. Just about everything that needs to be done for you and the baby will be done in this room. They will take the baby to the nursery for a little while to give her a bath and take blood, but then she'll be back in the room with you. Unless, of course, she has problems that we can't deal with here, but we're not going to worry about that." The nurse pushed some buttons on the machine next to the bed. "I'm going to take your blood pressure. It was a little high in the ambulance on the way here. Hopefully, it's gone down. If it hasn't we're going to need to try to get it down before you can have an epidural, okay?"

"Okay," Patty said.

She still hadn't let go of my hand, and I was glad. I think I needed her to hold on to my hand for my sake. I was feeling overwhelmed by everything that was happening. The room phone rang making me jump. I quickly answered it. "Hello."

"Theresa! Thank God!" Mandy said. "We've been trying to call both of you. What is going on? Daria said that Caleb Dalton pushed Patty down into a ravine and she had to be taken to the hospital."

"That's right. Patty's water broke when she fell, and it bruised her back. We called an ambulance because we were afraid she and the baby were hurt. They are both okay, according to the doctors. But Patty is definitely going to have the baby tonight," I explained.

"Is she able to talk?" Mandy asked.

I looked at Patty, who was looking at me questioningly. "Yes. Here she is." I handed the phone to Patty. "It's your mom."

"Mom," Patty said and started crying when she heard her mother's voice.

I retook her hand and listened as Patty asked how far away they were.

Elizabeth handed me tissues to give to Patty, who took them and wiped her eyes and nose. When she handed the phone back to me, she said, "They are in Riverton. They are dropping your dad's truck off at his garage, and then they will be headed this way."

"That'll take an hour or so." I looked at the nurse. "Will they have time to get here?"

"More than likely," Elizabeth said. "Even though you're over halfway dilated, we probably still have a few hours."

Patty gripped my hand as another contraction came. I looked up and watched the monitor as the line rose with the contraction. The nurse looked too. "Wow that was a pretty strong one. I'll check you again before I leave."

I watched Patty's face as she tried to breathe through the pain. It was an awful thing to see, this beautiful young woman's face reflecting the pain she was feeling. I wished there was something I could do to make this easier for her. When she released her grip, I stroked her hand. She smiled up at me.

I knew that I had been slowly falling for her even though I'd been trying hard not to. I didn't think she felt I was anything more than a friend, but right now I was head over heels, and there was nothing I could do. Even though she had told the staff that I was her girlfriend, I knew it was nothing more than a way to convince them to let me be in here with her. I was thrilled that she wanted me in here instead of Daria. Patty could have asked Daria to with her and said Daria was her sister. But, Patty had wanted me here and I was honored and thrilled.

Chapter Twenty-one
Patty

Theresa probably doesn't realize how much I need her here with me. Right now she's looking at me with a little fear and something more profound, like maybe love. And, I need someone to show me that kind of affection right now because I'm terrified.

Of course, I wouldn't really know what it would be like to be looked at with real love, not from anyone but my parents. She seems to sense that I'm reading her expression and turns away shyly.

God, I want to grab her and kiss her, just like I did in front of Destiny the other day. It had stunned everyone, including me. I'd done it to shut Destiny up when she started saying I'd gone queer. I still haven't found the words to honestly describe the sense of euphoria that kiss made me feel.

Theresa had smiled triumphantly at Destiny to go along with my story, but after she helped me into her truck, she didn't say five words all the way to my house. Of course, I hadn't had much to say either.

Her lips had been warm and soft, so unlike any of the guys I'd kissed. And there had been something more. It sounds cliché to say it was electric, but it had been.

I gripped her hand tightly as another contraction started.

"That was another good one," the nurse, Elizabeth said.

I tried to focus on my breathing as I listen to the baby's heartbeat. It picks up its pace with each contraction like she's working as hard as I am.

When the contraction passed, I relaxed and released Theresa's hand. I watched the nurse make some notes on the computer. "The contractions feel like they are getting closer together," I said. I know that's what is supposed to happen, but everything I'd been taught told that this whole process would start more gradually. I'd been having contractions pretty steadily all morning, and I'd been a little worried that I might be going into labor. After I fell and my water broke, the contractions became much stronger and closer together very quickly."

"Yes, the contractions are getting much closer together," Elizabeth observed and moved to the end of the bed.

The other nurse, Reina, who I could already tell that I wasn't going to like, moved to the end of the bed with Elizabeth and watched as Elizabeth checked me.

"Sorry," she said. "I know that hurts, but we need to see what's happening. You've dilated more; you're almost to six. That's good. Things are moving along nicely. I'll let the doctor know."

"Can I get something to drink?" I asked feeling extremely thirsty.

"I'm afraid not," Elizabeth said. "I can get you some ice chips, but you can't have anything to eat or drink just in case we have to go to surgery." She went to the computer and looked up something. "When they brought you into the emergency room, you said you hadn't had anything to eat since eleven this morning, is that right?"

"Yes," I said and sucked in another breath as another contraction came.

"Okay, good." She patted my knee and then picked up the phone she had laid next to the computer and started texting. Apparently, this was how the nurses and doctors communicated with each other now. After she read the responses, she said, "I'm going to go get some paperwork for you to fill out and I'll get you some ice chips." Turning to Theresa, she asked, "Would you like to have something to drink? We have Sierra Mist, Pepsi, and Diet Pepsi."

Theresa was surprised by the question and said, "I guess Sierra Mist."

"Okay," Elizabeth smiled and patted my knee again. "I'll be back in just a little bit."

Reina left with her, thankfully. I didn't like her attitude at all. Theresa was looking scared, and I reached out for her hand.

"I don't know how you are handling all this so calmly," she said. "I am totally freaking out."

I laughed. "I'm not as calm as I appear. I'm terrified that my fall did something to Mattie. Do you know what happened to Caleb?"

"I think some of the guys grabbed him for Officer Craig, but I wasn't paying any attention. I was too worried about you," Theresa said.

"I'm so glad you are here," I said squeezing her hand.

"Really?" she asked. "Are you sure you wouldn't rather have Daria in here? I think she and her boyfriend are in the waiting room."

"Yes, I'm sure. We hadn't had a chance to talk about this, but I wanted you to be here with Mom and me when Mattie was born. I like you," I said. "I like you a lot."

Theresa blushed. "I like you too."

Another contraction came, and once again I gripped her hand. I felt like I was about to break it.

"God, you have a strong grip," she said as she winced.

When the contraction passed, I said, "I'm sorry. You know, it just occurred to me that you might not even want to be here for all this. As I said, we didn't get to discuss it."

She kept hold of my hand and took her other hand to caress my cheek. "I'm honored that you want me to be here. I'm thankful I was with you at the graduation practice. I would have been beside myself if I was having to sit in the waiting room wondering what was happening in here with you."

I took my free hand and put it over her hand that was on my face. "I'm glad you feel that way. I would be even more terrified than I already am if you weren't here with me." I looked up at the clock on the wall by the door. "I hope Mom gets here in enough time. She really wanted to be with me when Mattie was born."

"I'm sure they are getting close," Theresa assured me. "And the doctor talked like they have time."

Tensing with the next contraction, I gripped both of her hands this time. "Yeah, but, my contractions are getting closer together."

The phone rang making both of us jump.

She reached for the phone, and I grabbed the bars on the bed as I tried to keep from crying out with the pain.

"It's Daria," Theresa said. "You want to talk to her?"

I nodded, and Theresa said into the phone, "She will when the contraction passes."

When it did pass, I motioned for her to give me the phone. "Hey," I said letting out a breath.

"Are you having the baby soon?" Daria asked.

"Yes," I said. "She's definitely going to be here soon."

"Will they let me come back there?"

"I don't know," I answered. "The hospital is apparently very strict about who gets to be here these days."

"It's probably because of the baby kidnappings," Daria said. "I've read stories about the father's families trying to take the baby from the hospital when they weren't allowed to see the baby because of fighting between the parents. It's scary nowadays."

"Thanks, that's just what I needed to hear," I said sarcastically. "Do you know what happened to Caleb?"

"They took him to jail," Daria answered. "Three guys grabbed him and wrestled him to the ground and held him there until Officer Craig could get cuffs on him, and then they put him in Officer Craig's patrol car. Principal Whipple was pissed. I've never seen him that mad. He said the school was going to press charges against Caleb. Even Destiny was freaking out. She couldn't believe he pushed you down like that with you being pregnant and about ready to pop."

"Good, I hope he gets what he deserves this time," I said.

"Do they think he hurt the baby?" Daria asked.

"I don't think so, but the doctor requested an ultrasound machine so she can to look at the baby," I said.

The door opened, and Elizabeth led a guy in with a cart that had the ultrasound machine on it.

"I gotta go," I told Daria. "They are here with the machine."

"Okay, I've got your phone. I talked to your mom a little bit ago. They were about a half an hour or so away," Daria said.

"Good. Are you going to hang out there for a while?" I asked.

"Yeah, we're going to stay at least until the baby is born, so we'll know you and the baby are okay."

"Good, I'll ask the nurse about who is a allowed to come back. But, if they won't let you, I'll have Theresa call you as soon as Mattie gets here," I said.

"Yeah, and later, you'll have to tell me about this Theresa thing," Daria said.

I blushed and said, "Bye."

Theresa took the phone and hung it up. Reina handed Theresa the cup of ice and the Sierra Mist. She held the cup for me so I could take out a piece of ice and put it in my mouth. The cold, wet ice felt good.

Dr. Denton came in a few minutes later. "Okay, let's see what's going on." She put up the stirrups. "Let's check you first and see how close we are."

Theresa was looking at me when I gritted my teeth as the doctor pushed her fingers into my womb. She felt around and frowned.

"What?" I asked.

"I'm not sure if we're going to have time for the epidural. You're completely effaced and dilated to seven."

I started having another contraction.

The doctor stood and took off her gloves. She turned to Elizabeth. "Pull up the history of the contractions for the last thirty minutes."

Looking at the clock again, that read five p.m., I realized that it had been almost four hours since I'd been put in the ambulance. There had been so much happening that I didn't know how much time had passed. I turned to Theresa. "Try to call Mom and see how close they are."

"Okay," she said and picked up the phone.

"You have to dial nine to get an outside line," Reina said.

"Thank you," Theresa said, smiling at the woman, who did not return her smile.

Theresa frowned and turned away. She dialed Mom's number and then took my hand in hers. Her thumb gently stroked the back of my hand until another contraction hit me and I grabbed her hand hard, making her wince.

"Hello, Mandy," Theresa said through gritted teeth.

Mom must have asked if she was okay, because Theresa said, "Patty is having a contraction, and she has my hand." Theresa nodded. "Yep, they are very close together. The doctor talks like it's going to be real soon." She looked down at me. "Your mom says you can't have the baby until she gets here."

"Well, she better hurry up," I said she said as she squirted a blob of the gel they used to help with the ultrasound onto my stomach.

"Okay, I'll tell her," Theresa said and hung up. "She said they are about fifteen minutes away."

"Good, she might get here in time after all," Dr. Denton said.

Theresa watched in fascination as the doctor put the probe on my stomach and the picture of the baby came up on the screen. She looked away as the doctor moved it to my pelvic area, but then looked back to the screen.

"Good," Dr. Denton said. "The umbilical cord is not near the baby's neck." She moved the probe around some more and then said, "Yep. Everything looks good." Her phone buzzed, and she pulled it out of her pocket. "Dr. Benote," she said into the phone. "She's already at more than seven, so if we're going to do the epidural we need to do it now."

She listened to what he was saying, but I stopped paying attention as the worst contraction so far came over me. I screamed out with the pain.

"Wow," Dr. Denton said after I'd settled back down. "Dr. Benote is on his way."

"Okay," I said weakly. I was completely spent after that one. I felt like my hips and stomach had been attached to some torture device, the pain was so severe that time, and my back was aching. "Can't you give me something in my IV?"

"No, we can't, hon," Dr. Denton said. "I know you're in a lot of pain, but there's not much we can do at this point. You'll just have to keep trying to breathe through the contractions."

Mattie's heartbeat picked up, and I could feel the next contraction building. It hadn't even been a minute it seemed.

The ultrasound machine was moved, and the nurses started getting things ready for the birth. A large black man in scrubs came into the room. "Are we ready?" he asked.

"Yes," I hissed as another contraction ripped through me. "Arrrrgh!" I cried.

Theresa held onto my hand tightly and urged me to breathe, as did Dr. Denton and the nurses. Dr. Denton put on another pair of gloves. She moved to the end of the bed and began examining me again. Turning to look at Dr. Benote, she said, "We won't have time. She's at nine, and I can feel the crown."

"What's that mean?" Theresa asked.

"That means this baby is coming," Dr. Denton said.

"Okay," Dr. Benote waved to everyone in the room. "Congratulations," he said to me.

There was a flurry of activity in the room, but I couldn't focus on anything but the pain. It had been steadily building to the unbearable point. The tears came as another contraction gripped my body.

Elizabeth, Reina, and Theresa helped me sit up so they could put pillows under my lower back. The bed was raised, and I was in the position to have the baby.

Theresa looked completely terrified. I think my screaming was what was doing that, but there was no help for it. The pain was too much.

"Okay," Dr. Denton said. "She is all the way into the birth canal, and I know you're feeling the urge to push, but you need to wait and push with the contraction."

I could only nod. I wanted my mother here. I wanted this baby out. I wanted the pain to stop.

"Okay, here we go," the doctor said as I felt the contraction building. "Now, push!"

I did what she said and pushed as hard as I could until I couldn't anymore, and the contraction passed.

"Good. You did good," Dr. Denton said. "Now, this time, you need to push harder. Her head's almost out."

The contraction came, and I pushed as hard as I could. I was hurting so bad and wanted to stop, but the doctor, the nurses, and Theresa kept urging me on. Finally, they let me breathe for a second.

"This is it," Dr. Denton said. "This time we're going to push her out. Ready?"

I just nodded as I saw Mom slip into the room. The contraction came, and I pushed as hard as I could, and I felt the baby slide out. Within seconds, she let out the sweetest little cry.

"Congratulations," Dr. Denton said. "She's perfect."

I started crying as the doctor turned to Theresa. "You want to cut the cord?"

Theresa looked at Mom and me wide-eyed. I smiled, and she turned back to the doctor and nodded.

Dr. Denton handed her the surgical scissors and said, "Anywhere between the clamps."

I heard the snip of the scissors and watched the doctor bring my naked baby over and lay her on my chest. Tears were flowing down my cheeks as I said, "Hello Matilda Marie McNeal."

Mom was next to me, crying as she kissed Mattie's head. "She's beautiful."

"Yes, she is," Theresa said as she stroked the baby's tiny arm. I noted that Theresa was crying too.

This was the most amazing moment of my life.

Chapter Twenty-Two
Theresa

I cannot believe that I just witnessed a child coming into the world. I cut the umbilical cord! The whole experience has been amazing, overwhelming and surreal. The pediatric team in the room took the baby to the warmer and put a diaper on her while Patty's doctor and the nurses helped rid her of the afterbirth. Mandy and I both focused on the baby while that was happening.

My heart is beating so hard. I feel like it might burst out of my chest. This experience was something I never expected to have. I knew I wasn't going to give birth to a child, but it had never occurred to me that I would meet someone who would want me in the room with them while they gave birth.

Patty told me she liked me a lot. Her wanting me to be here for the birth of her daughter, propelled my feelings for her over the moon. Looking at Mattie, now I understand what Dad meant when he said he fell in love with me the first time he laid eyes on me. I feel that way about little Matilda Marie McNeal.

Stroking Mattie's super soft skin right after she was born had been entirely mesmerizing, and then she had wrapped her tiny fingers around one of mine. There are no words to describe how I felt at that moment.

I'd looked into Patty's eyes when Mattie grabbed my finger, and she smiled at me so lovingly. It was the most amazing moment of my life.

Looking around I noticed a chair off in the corner away from all the activity. I sat down in it for a moment to get a grip on myself because I was feeling dumbfounded by all the emotions swirling around in my head.

Mandy came around to where I was sitting. "Are you okay?"

I looked up at her unable to hide my tears. "A little overwhelmed."

Mandy leaned down and hugged me. "Yes, isn't it is amazing?"

"Mattie is so beautiful," I said. "They are both so beautiful."

Mandy gave me another hug and then leaned back to look into my eyes. "Yes, they are." She smiled and then stood to get me a tissue from the box on the portable tray.

I took the tissue and wiped my eyes. The doctor finished with Patty, and they gave the baby back to her. I stood and went to the side of the bed. Patty took my hand and brought it to her lips. She kissed my knuckles and said, "Thank you for being here for me."

"Thank you for letting me be here," I said, smiling down at her and knowing she could see all the love I was feeling for her. I stroked the baby's downy hair. "She is so precious."

"Yes," Patty agreed.

Mandy was on the other side of the bed. She kissed Mattie's head and then took a picture of the three of us. "I'm going to send this to Richard. I don't think they will let him in since he's not family."

"He is," Patty said. "I told the paramedics that Theresa was the father so they would let her ride to the hospital with me, and he's her father."

Mandy laughed. "Well, maybe we can get them to let him come back for a few minutes then."

"Can you send the picture to Daria too," Patty asked. "She and Robbie are in the waiting room."

"Yes, I saw them when we raced up to the desk. Thank God we already had me on the list to be able to come back here. Those clerks at the desk were like drill sergeants and were not allowing anyone into the maternity ward. How'd you get the nurses to let her stay? I'm sure they guessed she wasn't really the father."

Patty looked at me and blushed. "I told them she was my girlfriend."

I blushed and stroked the baby's hair again.

"Well, it must have worked," Mandy said.

I could feel her studying me. She had to have been wondering if we really were a couple and how it had happened right under her nose.

The nurses, Elizabeth and Reina, came into the room and told Patty they were going to clean her up while the baby went to the nursery so the pediatrician could look at her. That was my cue to get out of the room for a few minutes. "I'm going to go out and have a cup of coffee with Dad. You want me to bring anything back with me?" I asked Patty and Mandy.

Patty turned to Elizabeth. "Do I have any restrictions now?"

"No, but I'm afraid you missed dinner. We can get something for you if you want. Or your girlfriend can get you something from the cafeteria," Elizabeth said.

Something about the way the nurse, Reina was looking at us must have set Patty off because she pulled me down to her and kissed me lightly on the lips before saying, "Could you get me a sandwich and some sweet tea, Babe."

"Sure," I said, blushing to my dark roots as I saw Mandy staring at me with a raised eyebrow. Quickly, I left the room and headed to the nurses' station for directions to the waiting room. When I got to the waiting room, Dad, Daria, and Robbie greeted me. "How are Patty and the baby?" Daria asked.

"They are great. Mattie is beautiful. She looks just like Patty," I said truthfully.

"Thank God," Daria said. "Are they going to let us see her?"

"I don't know," I said. "The hospital apparently has strict rules, but they were taking the baby to the nursery for a little bit. Maybe you'll be able to see her through the window. Did you get the picture from Mandy?"

Daria's phone chimed, and she looked down at the message. "Just now! Look at her! Oh, my God! She is so precious!"

"Awww," Robbie said smiling over Daria's shoulder at the baby.

Dad's phone buzzed, and he looked at his message. "Yep. She sure does look like Patty."

"I'm going to get Patty something to eat. You want to go to the cafeteria with me?" I asked Dad.

"Yes," he said putting his arm around me. "I need some coffee."

"Me too." I turned to Daria and Robbie. "You guys want to join us?"

"Nah, we'll wait here," Daria said.

On the way to the cafeteria, Dad asked, "How are you?"

"Shaken and amazed," I admitted.

"I bet," he said and turned to look at me. "You look pretty smitten in that picture Mandy sent me."

"Yes," I said putting my arm around his waist and leaning my head on his shoulder. "I'm afraid I may be in over my head."

He squeezed me. "It'll be okay. I think the feeling is mutual. I hear Patty told everyone back there that you were her girlfriend. When did that happen?"

"Today," I answered.

"No, I mean when did you start being in a relationship?"

I stopped just outside of the cafeteria and looked at Dad. "Today. We have been becoming closer friends, and she kissed me in front of a bunch of people at the high school one day, but that was to make a point. We've not talked about having anything more, but today she told the paramedics that I was the baby's father when they hesitated to let me ride with them. When we got here, and the nurses questioned me being in the room, Patty told them I was her girlfriend."

"So you two haven't really crossed that line?" Dad asked.

"No," I said and started walking toward the cafeteria again. "Patty told me today that she likes me a lot, and she kissed me before I left the room, but I think it was because this one nurse was giving us dirty looks."

"What did Mandy say?" Dad asked.

"Nothing. She just raised her eyebrow and gave me a questioning look."

There were only a few people in the cafeteria, so we were able to get our drinks and Patty's sandwich quickly. We sat down at one of the tables to drink our coffee.

"So what do you think will happen now?" Dad asked.

"I have no idea," I admitted. "But, Patty and I are definitely going to have to talk. I think she likes me like I like her, but I'm not sure."

Dad nodded at sipped his coffee. "I think you're right. I've seen her watching you. She just might be afraid."

Nodding, I said, "Once we get her and the baby home, I'll figure out a way to talk to her about what's going on between us."

"I just don't want to see you get hurt," Dad said.

"Me either," I agreed.

Chapter Twenty-three
Patty

Having to go to the bathroom woke me from the deepest sleep I think I've ever had. I opened my eyes and looked around the hospital room. Mattie was sleeping peacefully in her crib next to my bed. Theresa was sleeping on the couch next to the window, and Mom was asleep in the recliner next to the bed. I could see that it was dark outside. The clock on the wall read three a.m. I looked back to Mom and Theresa and wondered which one of them had fed Mattie at the last feeding. I had heard her crying. It seems that I remember Mom telling me she would feed her and for me to go back to sleep.

My bladder was demanding to be emptied, so I called the nurse. Elizabeth, who had just started her twelve-hour shift when I arrived at the hospital yesterday afternoon, came in the room.

"Need to use the bathroom?" she asked quietly.

"Yes," I whispered, not wanting to wake up Mom or Theresa. I knew they were almost as exhausted as I was after yesterday's drama.

It would seem that Caleb pushing me into the ravine hadn't done anything more than bruise my lower back and tailbone. When the doctor and I talked about when my contractions had started, it seems that I'd been headed to labor all day yesterday. The fall on my rump had only added to my pain and maybe pushed the labor along a little quicker than it would have come naturally.

At any rate, my beautiful little girl was perfectly healthy. Depending on the way things go will be released either later this afternoon, or first thing tomorrow. Mom will have to go back to Riverton this morning and get the car seat before we can go home. She and Richard had raced to Paducah without giving a thought for anything I'd need for the baby. Which was entirely okay, considering that all they knew was that I'd been pushed down a ravine by a maniac and rushed to the hospital.

The nurse helped me back to bed just as Mattie was starting to wake up for a feeding. After I was in bed, Elizabeth brought Mattie to me and brought me one of the pre-made bottles. Mattie looked up at me with her dark blue eyes that I knew would change later. Caleb's eyes were a sky blue, but I was hoping she would have green eyes like mine. Her hair was a light shade of red. Caleb had blond hair so her hair might be a little lighter than mine, but I was hoping it would be the same shade of auburn that Mom and I both had.

I put the nipple to her lips, and she sucked hungrily. I had been very torn about breastfeeding. My breasts had always been small, even during pregnancy they didn't get very big, but I was worried I wouldn't be able to produce enough milk to feed her. Listening to the soft sounds she made as she hungrily sucked the formula down, I think I made the right decision.

This moment was so precious. One of many I knew was to come. Right now there was no one but my daughter and me. The way she looked up at me, so trusting, filled me with love. I wish we could stay in this moment forever.

I called Elizabeth when I was done feeding and spending time with her. They didn't want me to walk with her by myself yet because of the pain medicine they were giving me. The doctor was afraid I'd be a little off balance.

"I wish I wasn't so tired. I would keep right on holding her," I told Elizabeth.

"She certainly is precious," Elizabeth said taking the baby.

"That must be the best part of being a maternity nurse. You get to see and hold all these beautiful babies."

"It is," Elizabeth agreed. "I'm glad I get to help be a part of babies coming into the world." She made sure Mattie was tucked into her blankets nice and tight. "Do you need anything before I go?"

"Just some water," I said. "I feel like I have cotton mouth."

"It's the pain medicine. It does that. We'll gradually take you off that throughout the day," she said.

"Do you think we'll get to go home today?"

"It's hard to say this early. It will depend on how much bleeding you have. How well the baby keeps her heat, or if she's jaundice. There's still a lot to be watched for, but she seems to be doing really well. Honestly, if I were you, I'd rather stay another day just to keep resting," Elizabeth said.

I sighed. "Well, I'm supposed to graduate from high school tomorrow, so I was hoping we'd be able to go home today."

Elizabeth smiled, but I could see the tinge of sadness in her eyes. I'm sure she saw situations like mine all the time. "All we can do is hope for the best. You get some more rest, and I'll be back to check on you before my shift ends."

"Okay," I said and rolled over to go back to sleep.

Chapter Twenty-four
Theresa

The sun shining through the curtains woke me. I was facing the back of the couch and the sunshine was reflecting off the lining of the thick curtains right into my eyes. Squinting, I rolled over onto my back and looked around the room.

"Good morning," Mandy said quietly.

"Morning," I whispered and looked over at Patty, who was curled on her side facing us and sleeping soundly.

Mandy followed my gaze and grinned. "She's always been adorable when she's asleep."

I sat up. The smell of coffee brought my eyes to Mandy's cup. "Where'd you get that?"

"Cafeteria," she said. "They opened at five. I went down and had breakfast and brought this back with me."

"That sounds good," I said, stood and stretched. I ran my hands through my hair and straightened my clothes. My jeans looked okay, but my red t-shirt was wrinkled. There was not much I could do to make myself more presentable.

Mandy reached into her purse and pulled out a brush. "Here, this might help."

Smiling, I took the brush. "Thanks." I went into the bathroom, splashed water on my face and brushed my hair. When I came out, I felt a little better about how I looked. "Do you want anything?" I asked Mandy.

"No, I'm good, hon. I had one of their apple fritters. You might bring one back for Patty. They're her favorites."

"Okay," I said. I looked at Mattie sleeping peacefully in her crib. My God, but she is beautiful. I smiled at Mandy and quietly left the room. I'd been down to the cafeteria last night with Dad, so I knew how to get there. Walking through the halls and listening to babies crying told me that many more babies had been born yesterday and last night. Yesterday had been magical and terrifying. Helping Patty bring Mattie into this world had been amazing.

The feelings I'd had for Patty had been building, really since I first saw her four years ago. I'd thought she was beautiful the first time I saw her in the hallways at school. For the two years, we'd shared those corridors, I'd found myself watching for her. Even though I'd never approached her back then, I'd learned things about her through other people. I didn't even realize what the crush I had on her meant until Linda Dalton kissed me for the first time. After that, my focus had been more on Linda, but I'd still watched for Patty. Now, after two years of not seeing her, my crush had come back as soon as I'd laid eyes on her when Dad and I met Patty and Mandy for dinner.

Over the past two months, my feelings for Patty have grown even though I was trying to keep my yearnings under control. I still feel that being friends is all Patty wants even though she has kissed me twice and told the nursing staff that I was her girlfriend. Yesterday, sometimes when she was looking at me, it felt like it was more. Of course, it was a very emotional day for everyone, so the way she was looking at me could have just been a part of all that was happening. I know for me, it solidified my feelings for Patty. Regardless of whether or not what we have ever becomes romantic, I know I want to be a part of Patty and Mattie's life.

I'd never held a baby before and for that first experience to be with Patty's child had been all the more special. Mattie was a miniature Patty, and she stole my heart the moment her little eyes met mine. I understand what Dad had meant when he talked about me imprinting on him when I was born. I feel that way about Mattie. There is nothing I wouldn't do for that little angel or her mother.

Chapter Twenty-five
Patty

I woke to the smell of coffee and donuts. For a minute I thought I'd died and gone to heaven. Looking around the room and seeing Mom and Theresa talking, and then seeing Mattie sleeping in her crib, I realized I am in heaven. All the people I loved were in this room. I paused at that thought and looked at Theresa. Yes, I love her. It was weird that I felt that way. We'd become close over the past few months as she'd worked on our house. I have no doubt we will continue to be friends even after the job is done. But, I had always felt a tinge of something more than friendship with her.

I'd wondered if it might just be a little bit of curiosity on my part. Not that I didn't know any gay people, ironically most of my friends at school, except Daria, are sexually fluid. Daria is unashamedly heterosexual. One of my friends from art class had been trying to get me to go out with her, but it just seemed like a game to me. She was cute in an androgynous way, but I just wasn't interested in her. With Theresa, it wasn't let's go on a date feelings; it was let's hang out and enjoy each other's company.

"Well, look who's awake," Mom said and got up to get Mattie.

Theresa laughed. "You thought she was talking about you, didn't you?"

"Yes," I said a little indignant, but I understood.

Mom walked over to the recliner and sat down with Mattie. "I've already spent eighteen years with you; I'm getting to know this little angel now."

I smiled and shook my head thinking that my child was going to be so spoiled, but that was okay. She was also going to be much loved.

Theresa pushed the tray toward me with a cup of coffee and an apple fritter on it. "The coffee is probably a little cold. I can go get you some hot coffee if you want me to."

I sat up and raised the hospital bed. "Let me see how cold it is." I sipped the coffee that was perfect because I like mine a little tepid and sweet. "This is great. Thank you."

"You're welcome," Theresa said, smiling warmly at me.

I was a little surprised she was still here. When Richard left last night, I thought she would go with him, but Theresa had fallen asleep on the couch while Mom and Richard talked. Of course, I'd fallen asleep not long after she did, and when I woke with Mattie at midnight Richard was gone, but Theresa and Mom were still here, both asleep. Theresa would probably go home with Richard today, that is if he came back to get her. She might have to ride home with Mom, Mattie and me. That is if they let us leave today.

The room phone rang startling everyone. Theresa answered it. "Hello," she said. I could tell by the way the conversation was going; she was talking to her dad. After several minutes of discussing different jobs, Theresa ended the call. "Dad got a hotel room in town last night rather than drive all the way home. He's going to come by in a little bit to pick me up. If you want we can call him around ten-thirty and have him stop and pick up some food for everyone."

"That sounds good," I said. "I feel like I could eat a horse." Picking up the apple fritter and taking a bite out of it, I moaned at how good it was. "Thank you for getting this for me."

"Your mom suggested it. She said they are your favorites," Theresa said.

"They are. These and cream stuffed chocolate eclairs," I said.

"I'll keep that in mind," Theresa said with a smile. She leaned down to look at Mattie, who was sucking on the nipple of the bottle of formula. "She's so beautiful."

"Yes," Mandy agreed. She took the bottle out of Mattie's mouth and put the baby on her shoulder to burp her.

We spent the rest of the morning taking turns playing with Mattie. Watching Theresa with Mattie was delightful. Theresa seemed so nervous about holding my tiny daughter, but she also seemed to be completely taken with the baby. She stared into Mattie's bright eyes as she fed her, and I was a little jealous of Mattie having Theresa's complete attention.

I wonder if Theresa and I will move beyond the friendship we've developed. I don't know if that's what she wants.

Theresa's eyes found mine over the top of Mattie's head, and she smiled at me. It warmed me all the way through my body. I have never had someone make me feel so cared about with a simple look.

Dr. Denton came by to check on me. She said I'd done well with delivery and gave me instructions on how to care for myself over the next six weeks until I saw her again. The pediatrician on call came in to check on Mattie. She was doing well, but they would keep an eye on her to make sure she didn't become jaundice.

The day shift nurse, Sarah came in and helped me take a shower. I'd put in an order for fried chicken with Richard, so when he arrived after I'd finished my shower, he had a bucket of Kentucky Fried Chicken for us all to share.

It was interesting how we felt like a family, Richard, Mom, Theresa and me. Richard cooed over the baby and held her for a little while before he announced that he and Theresa needed to get back to Riverton.

Theresa was hesitant to go, but she said, "I'll call later to see what the verdict is about you coming home today."

"Okay," I said. "Are you going to come back if they keep me?"

She smiled shyly, and I noted that Mom and Richard saw it too. "If you want me to."

"I do," I said and saw Mom and Richard exchange a look. I didn't care. I'd been through so much in the past year. Here was someone whose company I enjoyed, so I wasn't going to let Mom's concerned look stop me from asking Theresa to come back.

Theresa leaned across me to kiss Mattie on the head. "See you later, little angel." She smiled at me, and I almost pulled her down for a kiss, but I thought that might be a bit much for Mom. She didn't see me kiss Theresa yesterday in front of the nurse, or if she did; she didn't say anything about it.

"Get some rest," Theresa instructed, and then turned and followed her dad out of the room.

Mom waited until they had been gone for a few minutes before asking, "What's going on with you two?"

"Nothing, yet," I said.

"What do you mean nothing yet?" Mom asked.

"I like her, a lot. I don't know what it means exactly, but it's just the way I feel, and she likes me too, but I don't know if it's romantic or just friendship. If nothing else, I think we're going to be really close friends. I enjoy being with her," I said.

Mom studied me for what seemed like forever before finally saying, "I just don't want you to get hurt."

"I don't think Theresa will hurt me, not intentionally anyway," I said.

Mom frowned but then agreed. "I don't think she would either."

Fortunately, any more talk about my feelings for Theresa were cut off by the arrival of Mom's parents. I'd never been very close with my Grandma and Grandpa Miller. Partially because Mom wasn't close to them. Even though Mom's father had always been in construction, her parents had hoped she would marry someone with a stable job. It wasn't that they didn't like Dad, he just wasn't who they'd wanted for her. Mom's sister, Marion had married a lawyer and moved to Washington D. C. Grandma and Grandpa had always favored Marion, according to

Mom. It seemed to be true to me because they went to see Aunt Marion and her family often, but rarely came to see us and we live just a couple hours away from them.

They were also pretty religious so the fact that I was pregnant with an illegitimate child did not go over well with them. I'm actually pretty surprised they are here to see her.

Chapter Twenty-six
Theresa

Dad and I stopped by a gas station on the way out of town, and I got a root beer to drink on the way home. He got his usual sweet tea. We didn't say much to each other for the first few miles, and then he asked, "So, how strong are these feelings you have for Patty?"

I didn't answer right away, but I knew I couldn't lie to him. He'd see right through it. "Pretty strong."

He nodded and drove for a while longer. "I'm not sure how Mandy is going to feel about that," Dad said.

"I know. I've been worried about it. I'm not sure Patty feels the same way about me, but I know we like each other a lot. I don't know if it's romantic for her, but I promise I'm going to keep things on a friendship level, at least until I finish the job for Mandy."

"That's a good plan," Dad said. "I haven't talked to Mandy about it. I know she doesn't care that you're gay, but it's different when it's your child who has already been through so much."

Sighing, I said, "That's part of what I'm worried about with Patty. I don't know if she's just reacting to her hormones, or if she's developing feelings for me, or what, but I'm going to take it very slowly. I don't want to hurt her, and I don't want to get hurt again either."

"Fair enough," Dad said and went silent for a while before asking, "So how is the job coming?"

"It's going great. We're all but done on the inside. I'm going to do some punch out the first of the week, and then Mandy said she and Patty were going to do all the painting that's left. We've been working on the yard on and off, but now we'll focus on it and the outside of the house."

"Sounds good," Dad said. "I've got another job coming up soon, and I'm hoping you'll be able to run it."

"Sure," I agreed. "I'll make sure we're ready. There's so much that Mandy wants to do herself. She's only wanted us to do the things she didn't feel she could do on her own. Things like the painting and planting of small plants she wants to do herself, and that's shaving probably a week of the estimated time to complete the job."

"Of course, you know we will probably go help though, right?" he said with a grin.

"Yes, and since you've questioned me about my intentions. What's going on with you and Mandy?" I asked.

Dad grinned from ear to ear. "We're getting to know each other again. We're much more mature than we were all those years ago, but we're finding that we still have a lot in common even after all this time."

"That's great," I said. "You deserve to be happy."

He reached over and squeezed my shoulder. "Thank you, Sweetie. I want you to be happy too. I'm glad you're approaching this thing with Patty with a level head."

"Can I be honest about that?" I asked.

"Sure."

"I've had a crush on Patty since the first time I saw her when she started high school," I admitted. "I was just too afraid to approach her, and then Linda happened."

"Did you think she might be gay back then?" Dad asked.

"Well, my gaydar has never been very well developed, but I didn't talk to her, so there was no way for me to gage her. I think now she's uncertain herself. She had a bad experience with a guy so she might be more drawn to me because of that, but only time will tell if it's for real," I said.

"I think you're doing the right thing by taking your time," Dad said. "As you said, only time will tell, for either one of us."

"Hey, you want to help me with a big surprise for Patty?" I asked, an idea forming in my head.

"Sure," Dad said. "What do you have in mind?"

"You'll see." I grinned and called Jesus. I hadn't been sure what to give Patty for graduation and the birth of the baby, but now I knew what I was going to give her, but it was going to take a team.

Chapter Twenty-seven
Patty

I have never been so glad to see Riverton in my life. We are about fifteen minutes from home, and I can't wait to get there. It's still early in the day, and Mom said it's up to me whether or not I go to graduation, but I have no doubt that I will. I want to go to the high school and walk across that stage. I want to show everyone that I am strong and nothing that the Calebs, or the Destinys, of this world are going to do can hold me down.

Both sets of my grandparents were supposed to come too, but since Grandma and Grandpa Miller saw us this morning, they decided not to drive all the way to Riverton to watch me graduate. Grandpa McNeal was having health issues so they weren't going to get to come up. Mom said that we'd go down and see them this summer before we opened the bed and breakfast.

Mom is worried that I'm going to be too tired to make it graduation. The whole ceremony will probably last two or three hours, but I'm not worried about it. I'm going to take a nap while Mom watches Mattie and then I'll be ready.

When we pull in and see Richard's truck is in the driveway, I look over at Mom who looks puzzled too. I was a little peeved at Theresa because she didn't come back to the hospital last night like she'd promised. She said something had come up with a project and she had to take care of it. I wonder where she is now since her father is here to greet us.

Richard came out on the porch with a sheepish grin on his face. "We thought we had time to get everything done before you got here."

"Get what done?" Mom asked.

"You'll see," he said beaming.

Mom looked over the car at me as I got out. I shrugged, opened the back door, and took Mattie's car seat out. Picking up the car seat, that weighs a ton, I figure it shouldn't take too long to get the pregnancy weight off lugging this thing around. It's warm outside, but I still cover Mattie's head. I'm trying not to be one of those complete germ freaks around the baby, but it's apparently natural for new mothers.

I lug the car seat up the four steps to the porch and see that Theresa is inside the house. She's wearing a button-up, dark blue long-sleeved shirt and jeans, with the sleeves of the shirt, rolled up. She's shifting her booted feet nervously, and it makes me wonder what the two of them have done.

The first thing I notice is that the living room is now completely furnished. This is only a mild shock because I knew Mom had ordered the furniture. Apparently, it had arrived while I was in the hospital, and based on the cheesy grins on both Theresa and Richard's faces; they must have put them in the house for us.

I hear Mom, who's further in the house, say, "Oh my God! Patty come look!"

Theresa takes the car seat from me, her hand brushing mine as she does. "Go on. I've got Mattie."

I let her have the car seat and follow the direction of Mom's voice. She's in the room that she and I had been sharing. I stop dead in my tracks at the door. The bedroom has been finished. The walls and trim are painted the exact colors of soft peach and cream trim that I'd wanted. There was a full sized bed made of wood stained with cherry and a dresser and bureau to match. The bed was covered with a comforter that was cream colored with blue cornflowers on it. Next to the bed was an old-fashioned white wicker bassinet. Across the room was a baby bed made of wood that matched the rest of the furniture. I walked over to it with my hand to my mouth and saw that it even had a blanket set that matched my bed.

"Did you do this?" I asked Mom.

"I picked everything out, but I thought we had a few more weeks to set it up," Mom said. "Richard and Theresa are the ones who must have put this together." She turned to Richard, who was standing next to Theresa in the doorway. "None of this was here when I left for Paducah."

Richard nudged Theresa, who was looking down at her feet, with his shoulder. "Theresa wanted to have it ready for you when you got home, so she talked John and Jesus into helping us. We put it all together last night and this morning."

I went over and stood in front of Theresa and looked up into her dark eyes. "You are amazing. Thank you," I said and wrapped my arms around her neck and kissed her on the cheek. Turning to Richard, I hugged him and kissed his cheek too. "You too."

Mom came over and hugged Richard and then kissed him on the lips. "Thank you." She let him go to hug Theresa too. "This is absolutely amazing."

"Yes," I agreed. "This is the best gift you could have given Mattie and me, ever."

"Well, I didn't want you to have to worry about working around the baby," Theresa said, still being a little shy. "This way you won't have to worry about her being around any paint fumes."

"I know," I said and went over to the bassinet. I can even cover this with light netting to keep any dust away from Mattie while we're finishing the rest of the house."

"We're so close now, it's really not going to take more than a few weeks," Mom said. "Hopefully, by the time we're ready to start booking guests, Mattie will be passed the waking up at all hours of the night phase."

"Yeah, we might need to wait until she's past that stage before we start booking people," I agreed. Of course, I had some misgivings about having a bed and breakfast now that we have Mattie. But, it's Mom's dream, so we'll figure it out.

"Are you going to take a nap before graduation?" Mom asked.

"Yes," I said, feeling the long ride and being up with Mattie so much last night catching up with me.

"Well, we'll take Mattie in the other room so you can nap. I'll wake you up in a couple of hours so you can take a shower and get something to eat, and then we'll head to the high school," Mom said.

I turned and looked at her, trying not to show the fear I suddenly felt, "Do you think that Caleb will be there?"

"You don't have to worry about him if he is," Richard said. "Theresa and I will be there to watch over you and Mattie with Mandy."

"Thank you," I said, relieved. I looked over at Theresa who was bending down to check on Mattie. She turned and looked at me. It warmed me seeing her looking in on my daughter. I knew that I would never have to worry about Mattie, or Mom, with Theresa and Richard around.

Chapter Twenty-eight
Theresa

I have to admit I'm a little nervous about going to Patty's graduation. I'm so excited to be there for her, but I'm a bit apprehensive about what might happen if Caleb Dalton is there. I think the dude has lost his mind.

I also wondered if Linda would be there for Caleb. Having not seen her in more than two years, I'm curious as to whether or not she will show up, what she looks like now, and if she is really married as I've been told.

Shaking off my thoughts about Linda, I focus on the time at hand. Dad and I left for home after Patty laid down. We both got showers and changed for the graduation. I have a clothing dilemma. I want to look really good for Patty, but I have a limited wardrobe. Jeans and t-shirts are usually all that's required for my job. When I go out to bid a job, I typically wear nice jeans and a button-up shirt. I don't even have a pair of dress pants.

I finally decide on a black pair of jeans, a cobalt blue button-up shirt, and brown loafers. Looking at myself in the mirror, I realize this is as dressed up as I'll probably ever be. The outfit also reflects my butch lesbian identity, and I'm not ashamed of that. Truthfully, Patty needs to see that this is who I am and that I'm not going to change, not for her, or anyone else.

I met Dad in the living room. He had on a pair of beige dress pants, a light blue button-up shirt, and a tan blazer. I smiled. Yep, this was as dressed up as the two of us got.

"Ready?" he asked.

"Yes," I answered.

We went out and got into his midnight blue 1968 Ford Mustang. Dad wasn't big on fancy cars, but this was his one toy that he afforded himself, besides the camper and jet skis he had for summer trips to the lake. I loved this car. To me, the older cars like this were the best cars. If I were ever to decide I wanted something to drive besides my truck, which I honestly love, this would be the kind of car I'd get.

The high school was about thirty minutes from our house, and neither of us had said anything on the way there. Finally, Dad said, "You seem nervous."

"I guess I am a little," I admitted. "I haven't been back here since I graduated, other than when I picked up Patty for Mandy, and the day I was here with Patty and she went into labor. That last year of high school wasn't a happy time, and I know some of the people I went to school with have younger sisters and brothers, so I'm wondering how many of them I'm going to run into today."

"You mean, you're wondering if Linda Dalton is going to be there," Dad said knowingly.

"Yeah," I said quietly.

"You know, that is all a part of the past. You've come a long way in just a few years. Most of the people you went to school with are still in college. Very few of them are working and building a good reputation for themselves like you are, so don't let any of them make you feel uncomfortable. You should be proud of who you are." Dad had turned to look at me while he said it.

"Please watch where you're going," I said, seeing the side of the road getting closer.

He turned back to the road and corrected his driving. "You have nothing to be ashamed of, Theresa. Just because some of those fools had a problem with your sexuality doesn't mean anything anymore. That was high school; this is real life," he said. "Your happiness and success are all that matters. Don't give a second thought about what any of those people think."

I know he's right, but that doesn't ease my nervousness. I dealt with a lot of teasing and bullying that last year. I'd ignored most of it, but it still hurt that people who had thought I was cool when I was a jock had turned on me as soon as they saw me as less of a person.

Yeah, life was different now, and I probably make more money than most of the people I went to school with, but I'm still nervous about running into my former classmates. I know I shouldn't be, but that doesn't change the fact that I am.

When we got to the school and found a parking spot, Dad looked over at me and took my hand. "No matter what other people think, Theresa, I'm proud of you."

"Thank you, Dad. That means a lot," I said and meant it. Dad was my rock, and I knew he would always be there for me.

We made our way through the crowd of families vying for good seats while Dad texted

Mandy to find out where she was sitting. Dad stopped suddenly and turned to his left. I followed his gaze and saw Mandy standing up and waving at us. Dad made his way to Mandy with me following him.

"I saved you guys seats," she said and motioned to the empty seats next to her.

She had Mattie in her car seat in front of her. The little angel was sleeping despite all the noise going on around her. I envied her.

As I suspected, there were several of my former classmates here supporting their younger sisters and brothers. A few of the guys from my class had given me a nod and wave. I tried to focus on what Mandy was saying and not look around at the people around us. I knew I was looking for Linda in my subconscious. I don't know why. I guess to see her in her new role and give myself closure about what happened between us before I allowed myself to try to love again.

I know I'm falling in love with Patty more and more every day, which scares the shit out of me. I feel like she is feeling that way too, but she's a younger, previously straight, woman who may not be entirely ready for the lesbian lifestyle. Not that I really participate in any lifestyle, I just work and hang out with my dad. But, if things were going to happen between us, I am going to want to be open about it. I was forced out of the closet, but now that I'm out I'm not going back.

After sweeping the crowd, I turn back to Mandy, who is saying, "Patty is wearing the most beautiful dark green dress. I found it online a few months ago. I'd gotten it big enough to fit her while she was pregnant, so I had to take it in a little, but it looks amazing on her. It brings out the green in her eyes. She looks just beautiful."

"I bet she does," Dad was saying, and I was picturing Patty in a dark green dress. Of course, I think she would look beautiful in anything.

"How did she feel when she got up?" I asked.

"She was still pretty tired, but I figure after we get back home she'll go back to bed," Mandy said. She looked down lovingly at Mattie. "I don't mind watching the baby for her. I know Patty wants to spend more time with her, but she needs her rest too."

The principal walked up to the microphone on the stage and got everyone's attention. He said how thankful everyone was for the beautiful weather for today's ceremony.

It was a gorgeous day. There wasn't a cloud in the sky. It was about seventy degrees, which was a good temperature, not too cold or too hot. There was just the lightest of breezes. It was truly perfect.

We sat quietly and listened to all the speeches and clapped at the appropriate times. Finally, they started parading the students across the stage. I felt like all three of us were holding our breath, waiting to see if they were going to call Caleb Dalton. When they did, we looked at each other and shook our heads. I heard Mandy say quietly, "I knew that son of a bitch would get him out of jail for this."

Dad put his arm around her. "I suspected that too, but we'll snap Patty up as soon as this is over and get her away from him."

I noted that Mandy nodded, moved closer to Dad, and reached over and squeezed his knee.

When it came Patty's time to come up to get her diploma, the most of her classmates and a lot of the parents stood and cheered for her. That made me feel so good. At least most of them knew what had happened and what it meant that she had made it to the graduation.

Patty waved to them. Principal Whipple whispered something in her ear and gave her a tight hug, which brought tears to my eyes. Mandy had started crying when everyone stood up, and now she was crying in earnest. Dad produced a box of tissues that Mandy had apparently packed in the diaper bag. I took one too, and Dad put his free arm around me. This was such a beautiful moment for Patty, and I am so glad I was here to witness it.

An hour or so later, after the last of the speeches, and the students were pronounced to be graduates, everyone started searching out their loved ones. Dad packed Mattie's car seat as we made our way to Patty.

When we finally found her, Mandy wrapped her in a tight hug. "Oh, my baby girl. I am so proud of you."

"Thank you, Mom," Patty said and held her mother as they both cried. "I can't believe this day is finally here."

When Patty let go of her mom, she came to Dad and hugged him, and then turned to me. She kissed my cheek much as she had at the house earlier and hugged me tightly. "Thank you both for being here for me."

"It was an honor," I said, squeezing Patty to me. It felt funny hugging her without the large bump between us.

She looked up at me and smiled, making my heart do flip-flops in my chest. Yes, she had captured my heart. I could only hope she didn't break it.

I felt the tension coming from Dad and Mandy and looked up. Eric Dalton was approaching us with his wife, Betsy. Linda was with them, walking next to a handsome man, who appeared to be in his late twenties. He had a possessive hand on Linda's lower back. I felt like we were getting ready to be in a showdown as they lined up in front of us.

Eric Dalton smiled, showing his perfect white teeth. "I hear that you had an uncomplicated birth," he said to Patty. "I'm glad that your little fall didn't hurt you or the baby."

"I don't know who told you Patty didn't get hurt," Mandy said. "She was severely bruised and went into labor a week early."

Eric's smile didn't falter. "I just meant that Patty and the baby are both okay now."

"Yeah, we're fine," Patty snapped.

"So, does the baby look like Caleb," Betsy asked trying to peak at the baby, who miraculously was still sleeping.

"She looks like Patty. I don't know why you're worried about it. Your son signed papers relieving him of any parental responsibilities," Mandy said.

"I guess, I'm just curious," Eric said.

"Well, don't be," Patty said firmly. "My daughter is not your business."

"Well, I don't know," Eric said. "Now that we've given it more thought, maybe we should have a paternity test done, just to be sure."

"No," Patty said. "The chance for being a part of this child's life passed months ago. I won't let you have a role in her life now."

"You won't have a choice," Eric said firmly, his smile starting to fade.

Betsy, Linda, and the man Linda was with started looking uncomfortable as more people seemed to be noticing the standoff between the two families.

"Fine," Mandy said. "You want a paternity test. We'll get one, but that might negate some of the conditions of our original agreement."

Patty's head swung in her mother's direction. "What are you doing?"

"I've already talked to our attorney about this possibility," Mandy said, not taking her eyes off of Eric's. "In fact, it's been an ongoing conversation, especially since Caleb has attacked Patty several times."

"Is that right?" Eric snarled. "I've been talking to my attorney too."

Mandy said very calmly. "I'm not going to tell you any more about the discussions I've had with my attorney, but if a paternity test is what you want, we'll make arrangements."

Patty stood there staring at her mother open-mouthed. I slipped my arm around her and whispered, "She's bluffing, or she has something else up her sleeve. Give her a chance to explain later."

Patty turned to me with a surprised and fearful look on her face. I knew she was thinking what I was thinking. If the Daltons had proof that Mattie was Caleb's they might force visitation, which would be awful for everyone, especially Mattie. The Dalton's would try to brainwash her against her mother.

"Well, I didn't expect you to be agreeable," Eric said. "I'll have my attorney contact yours Monday, and we'll get the arrangements made."

Eric and Betsy walked off, and I noticed that Caleb was standing several feet away with sheriff deputies flanking him.

Linda and the man she was with stayed behind. She turned to me and said, "I see you have not changed your ways."

"Excuse me?" I asked.

She looked from Patty to me. "You are still living a sinful life. You should go to the conversion therapy camp I attended. They cured me of any inappropriate thinking and helped me become a good God-fearing woman." She turned to the man next to her. "That's where I met Justin. We're going to be married soon."

"Good for you," I said, thinking that I wanted to throw up. "But I'm fine with who I am."

Linda looked back at Patty. "You really should stay away from her. She will suck you into her perverted way of life and destroy you."

Patty pulled away from me, and I didn't know if I should step back or stop her, but I could tell by the look on her face, I was getting ready to see an example of that hot-headed temper that her mother said she could have.

"Who the hell do you think you are talking about her like that? You are the one who outed her when you didn't have to. You're the one who humiliated her and made sure that the rest of her senior year was the worst year of her life. Theresa loved you, and you dumped her like a hot potato when your father found out about you. Now, you dare to say that she's a pervert? You are the one who is sick, especially if you think that conversion crap really worked. Theresa is a beautiful, warm and funny woman, and I am glad she is a part of my life." Patty turned to me, took my face in her hands and kissed me on the lips, a lingering kiss that had my head spinning.

When she released me, I looked at Linda, whose face had gone white, and her shocked boyfriend. "Sick people," she said and stomped off to join her family with her boyfriend hurrying to catch up with her.

"She's just lucky I'm still recovering from giving birth, or I'd kick her ass," Patty growled.

"Patricia!" Mandy said but with a half laugh.

"Yeah, and what was that crap you were doing? Why would you agree to a paternity test now?" Patty demanded.

"The agreement we originally signed let Caleb get out of his paternal obligations, but it has a clause that says if the Daltons change their minds, they have to pay for all of your medical bills as well as pay child support based on Eric's income until Caleb gets a job. Our attorney and I have also been talking about suing the Daltons for pain and suffering caused by Caleb's attacks against you. You and I just haven't had a chance to talk about it," Mandy explained.

Patty stared at her mother in stunned silence. "What brought about that idea?"

"I was asking our attorney what we could do should Eric reverse his agreement, like he just did," Mandy said. "He told me about the clause in the agreement. He said he's sure that Eric thinks he can get around it, but none of the judges in our county like fathers who try to ditch their obligations. If it goes to court, the judges will most likely rule in our favor as far as the money goes. We have all seen how dangerous Caleb is. It is one of the reasons why he shouldn't have visitation at all, and his parents will only be allowed supervised visitation."

Patty shrugged. "Okay. We'll see what happens, but they are not going to get to take the baby anywhere without me."

"No, they won't," Mandy assured her.

"So, who's ready to go get something to eat," Dad asked rubbing his hands together.

"Are you kidding?" I asked. "Every restaurant in town is going to be packed."

"True," Dad agreed, a little disappointed.

"How about we buy some steaks and go cook them at your house on that nice big grill you have?" Mandy suggested.

"That sounds like a good idea," Dad said. He turned to Patty and me. "What do you guys think?"

"Steak does sound good," Patty said. "We'll just need to go to the house and get some more diapers and formula for Mattie."

"How about this, Richard and I will go to the store and get the supplies for dinner, and you and

Theresa go to the house to get what you need for Mattie?" Mandy suggested.

"Works for me," I said, glad to have time alone with Patty.

"Okay," Patty agreed too. "We'll meet you at Richard and Theresa's in a little bit."

We split up. Dad and Mandy headed for his Mustang. Patty and I went in search of Mandy's Civic.

"I think your mom just wanted to ride in the Mustang," I said as we walked.

"I think she just wanted to be alone with your dad," Patty laughed.

We were stopped by Daria and several other girls from Patty's class. Daria wrapped her arms around Patty and squealed. "I can't believe you made it."

"Me either," Patty admitted.

"Can we see the baby," one of the other girls asked.

"Sure," Patty said and lifted the blanket off the baby car seat.

Mattie was awake and looking around. Her little fists waving in front of her face until she got one in her mouth.

"Oh my God!" Daria exclaimed. "She's beautiful."

"Thank you," Patty said proudly.

The other girls cooed over her until Mattie started fussing.

"Well, that's our cue. We need to get her into the car, so I can start feeding her," Patty said.

All of the girls hugged Patty. Daria hugged me. "Keep her safe," she said in a quiet voice.

"I will," I promised.

The girls headed off calling out to other friends. I picked up the car seat and strapped it into the backseat while Patty got Mattie's bottle ready. I noticed a police car by the side of the school and watched as some officers put cuffs on Caleb and escorted him to the car. "Caleb really did get out just for the graduation," I told Patty. "There's cops over there taking him back to jail."

Patty followed the direction of my finger. "Good. That's where that son-of-a-bitch needs to be. You drive." She handed me the keys.

I took Mandy's keys and got into the driver's seat. I turned toward the backseat and watched Patty feed Mattie.

"What?" Patty asked.

"I just like watching you guys," I said.

"You're silly," she said with a smile.

"Well, I hope you like silly because I'm always going to be this way."

"I like silly," she said.

After she fed the baby and put her in her car seat, I started the Civic, and we headed back to Patty's house. Patty had moved to the front seat and took my hand in hers when I put it on the console between us. We drove the rest of the way to her house like that, and it felt perfect. I hoped that meant that we would be moving forward with this relationship because I really wanted to know where we were headed. Hopefully, we would talk about it soon.

Chapter Twenty-nine
Patty

When we got to Richard and Theresa's house, Mom and Richard were on the back patio getting the grill ready. They both had a glass of red wine and were talking animatedly. I wondered what they were talking about that was so interesting. When Theresa and I got closer, I could hear that they were talking about Florida.

We used to go as a family once every few years. I loved going to Florida and sitting by the ocean. I wasn't a big fan of playing in the water the way Mom and Dad had. I hated getting the salty water in my mouth.

Mom turned and waved at us as we approached. We'd walked around the house instead of going through it to get to the deck. The deck was set up for entertaining. It was enclosed with a railing that had seats built into it. There was also a glass table with an umbrella in the center that could seat four to six people.

Richard came over and took the car seat from me and put it on the table under the umbrella. Mom lifted the blanket I had over the car seat to shield Mattie's face from the bright afternoon sun.

"She is such an angel," Mom said and leaned down to kiss her on the forehead. Mattie's breathing didn't even change as she was sleeping so soundly.

Richard said, "I've got potatoes in the oven, a large salad made up, and we were just waiting for you girls to get here before we put on the steaks."

"Great, I'm starving," Theresa said.

"Me, too," I agreed. I hadn't eaten since I'd had breakfast at the hospital that morning.

I lifted the blanket back over Mattie so the gnats that were buzzing around wouldn't bother her.

"What do you guys think about watching a movie tonight?" Mom asked. "Richard's got a sixty inch screen and cable. We thought we'd try to find something all of us could watch together."

"Sounds good to me," Theresa said.

"Sure," I agreed. I wasn't real sure if I would be able to stay awake through a movie, but I did want to spend more time with Theresa. I watched her as she leaned casually against the deck railing. I don't think I would use the word beautiful to describe her, not in the typical definition of the term beautiful. I guess handsome would be a more apt description. Her dark brown hair lay at her collar with the slightest curve. It was parted just to the left of center and lay in soft layers. I found myself itching to run my fingers through it. She turned her dark eyes and captured mine, holding them for several seconds, until I realized Mom was watching us and I looked away.

Richard came back out of the house with the steaks. "Tee why don't you give Patty a tour of the house and get you guys something to drink."

"Do we get to have wine?" I asked grinning wickedly at my mother.

"No," Mom and Richard both said.

Theresa laughed. "That's okay. There's some sparkling grape juice in there we can have."

"I was just kidding about the wine," I said as Theresa led me through the back door that opened into the kitchen.

"I know," she said as she opened the refrigerator. "Did you want the sparkling grape juice, or would you rather have something else."

Looking over her shoulder, I spotted a pitcher of tea. "Is that sweet tea?"

"Yep. Want some?"

"Yes," I said and moved toward the table. The dining room and kitchen apparently doubled as a mud room as I noted two pairs of work boots sitting by the door. The kitchen was very simply decorated. The wood walls had pictures of nature scenes in frames.

After Theresa poured our glasses of tea, she said, "Let me give you the tour." Off the kitchen and dining room area was the living room. The front door was almost directly across the house from the back door and shared the wall with two large windows that looked out onto the front yard and driveway. The living room had wood walls like the kitchen and beige carpet. It was furnished with a recliner, couch, and oversized chair that were all a chocolate brown leather. Cherry end tables sat between the couch and each chair with a matching long coffee table in front of the couch. A large television screen hung on the wall opposite of the couch. The rest of the walls were decorated with antique tools. There was a door on the same wall as the television. Theresa opened the door slightly, and I peeked past it to see the clean bedroom with a queen-sized bed and a recliner, facing the doorway. I could see there was also a big screen television on this wall.

"Clearly your father's room," I said, noting the clothes tossed on the bed and the pictures of famous architecture.

"Yeah," Theresa said. "He's kind of a neat freak.

She closed the door and took me across the living room to another door that led to a room that was clearly her bedroom. It wasn't a feminine room, but it wasn't as masculine as her father's either. There were several trophies from high school on top of bookshelves, which were filled with books. This surprised me. I wouldn't have pegged Theresa as a reader. Her walls have a few family pictures on them. Mostly ones of her and her father, although there were a few of their family when it had been together.

The bed was made, but there were clothes strewn about. There were a couple of books on her nightstand and a half-full glass of water.

"I'm not that neat," Theresa said as she leaned against the door. She pointed to a doorway further into the room. "That's my bathroom if you need to use one. I never go into his bathroom. That's too private a space for me."

"Thanks, I wouldn't want to use his private bathroom either," I said and then pointed to a picture on the wall. It was of Theresa, her mother, father, and brother during what appeared to be happier times. "Where was this?"

She said, "That was in Panama City about four years ago. It was the last vacation we took as a family."

I studied the picture. Her mother looked unhappy. "Did she not like Florida?"

Theresa moved closer to me and looked at the picture. "Not really. She got too sweaty, too much sand, not enough shopping."

"You don't look anything like her," I noted.

"Thank God," Theresa said. "I'd hate to have that memory staring at me every morning in the mirror."

"Your brother doesn't look like either one of your parents," I said, studying the teen with dark blonde hair and a ruddy complexion.

"Mom said he looks like her grandfather," Theresa said. "He's definitely her son though. He's just like her, a snooty punk who needs his ass kicked."

Both my eyebrows shot up. "No love lost between the two of you, huh?"

"I can't stand him," Theresa said. "He's lazy. Never once did he set foot on one of Dad's jobs. The both of them always acted like it was beneath them to go to Dad's office or meet him at a job. I loved being on the job sites. I love seeing new houses develop from nothing, and taking places like your mom's house that were run down and turned them into something beautiful." She smiled at me. "I think her bed and breakfast is going to be a huge success."

"I hope so," I said. "She's always wanted to have one. It was something she and Dad had talked about doing with the house they bought shortly before he died. It would have been perfect because it was so close to the river that you could see it from the windows in the upstairs bedrooms."

"Well, in a way, he still helped her get her bed and breakfast," Theresa said. "He left her enough money to get started."

"That's true," I agreed.

I turned and was standing right in front of her. She was looking down at me, studying my eyes. I knew she wanted to kiss me, but was afraid. We stood there searching each other's eyes until my mother broke the spell that was working its way over us, leading to another kiss that might have been a really serious one. "Hey! Did you guys get lost?"

"No," I said smiling at Theresa's blush from us almost getting caught. "We were talking about the bed and breakfast and how successful she thinks it's going to be."

"You think so?" Mom asked, and when we moved into the living room, Richard was standing there with a chef's apron on.

"I do," Theresa said. "There's not a lot of places for people to stay out this way and we get a lot of travelers, fisherman, hikers and nature lovers who come through here. I think the fact that you've chosen to go a little more modern with your rooms and not as country, or historic, as some of the other bed and breakfasts in the area will draw a good amount of people. Not everyone is into old farmhouses with historic furniture. Some people want a homey place to stay where they aren't worried about spilling something on grandma's antique quilt."

"That is completely true," Richard agreed. "My brother came down a few years ago and stayed at a bed and breakfast about thirty miles from here. They said it was beautiful, but it was hard to relax because they felt like they were walking on eggshells the whole time they stayed there and constantly worried about breaking, or spilling something."

"Let's take this back outside," I suggested, realizing that the baby was by herself.

"Oh lord, yes," Mom agreed, realizing too that we'd left the baby outside.

I hurried out and peeked under the blanket. Mattie was sleeping soundly. Her soft breathing was a relief. Obviously, Mom and Richard couldn't be trusted to watch her for very long.

I sat down next to Mattie's car seat, feeling the length of the day quickly catching up to me. I wasn't sure if I was up to watching a movie, but I would stay if Mom wanted to stay.

Richard turned the steaks, and Theresa brought out plates, a pitcher of tea, and glasses. Mom brought the salad and potatoes out. Theresa went back for condiments, and I put Mattie's car seat on the ground at my feet.

The conversation about the bed and breakfast continued over dinner. Richard and Theresa were both very excited about it. Theresa encouraged Mom to go ahead and get the windows replaced with more secure and airtight ones. Richard also suggested making a driveway that went around to the back of the house, so the guests' cars were not on the street. I listened to them talk about the ideas and how to do it for the least amount of money. Mom didn't want to have to borrow money for the house if she could avoid it.

By the time dinner was over, I was worn out, but Mom was excited about watching a movie with

Richard and Theresa. Mattie woke up right as we were cleaning up, so I took her in the house, changed and fed her while everyone else cleaned.

When the cleaning was done, Richard came in and sat in the recliner. Mom sat on the couch close to Richard. I was already at the opposite end of the couch, so Theresa sat down in the chair closest to me. She produced and ottoman from the side of the chair and stretched her long legs out on it. I put my feet on the ottoman too and put Mattie on my chest as I kissed and cooed with her. She was still tired from all the work of coming into this world and didn't stay awake more than thirty minutes. I found myself dozing as I tried to watch the action flick Richard had talked Mom into watching. Normally I like action movies, but I was just too tired.

I snapped awake when Mom took the baby off my chest. "Sorry," Mom said. "I was afraid you'd drop the baby."

"Oh," I said sleepily and sat up.

"Why don't you go lay down on my bed," Theresa suggested. "Your mom can wake you when she's ready to go."

"I don't know," I said, looking over at Mattie who was asleep in Mom's arms.

"Go ahead, honey," Mom said. "It's been a long day for you."

"Okay," I said finally, stretching. "I'll take Mattie in there with me. She shouldn't wake up before you're ready to leave."

Mom handed my baby to me. "I'll come get you in a little bit."

Nodding, I turned to Theresa. "Thank you."

"No problem," she said.

Mattie and I went to Theresa's room, and I settled us on top of the comforter. I was hot and just wanted the blanket on my feet. I had Mattie in the middle of the bed so I knew she wouldn't be close to the edges. I lay with my nose close to her little head, so I felt her heat and smelled her sweet baby smell.

The next thing I knew, Mattie was fussing, so I got up and made her a bottle. I cuddled her into the crook of my arm while I fed her. Theresa's clock on her nightstand read almost midnight. Great. Mom had left me there, or they were still watching movies. There was some noise coming from the other room, so I decided that was the case.

Once Mattie was fed and changed again, I went back to sleep. I was so tired that I just barely noticed someone getting into bed with us.

Chapter Thirty
Theresa

I was surprised when Mandy sent me to wake Patty. She was still sleeping in my bed. After she'd went to my room to lay down last night, Mandy and Dad decided that Mandy and Patty would spend the night with us rather than go home so late. Mandy had joined Patty and Mattie in my bed and I had slept on the couch.

Mandy had gotten up with the baby at five this morning and started coffee for which Dad and I were very glad. We'd stayed up later than we normally would, but it had been fun watching movies with Dad and Mandy. The two of them were clearly enjoying each other's company. I felt like a third wheel, but I didn't think Mandy would like the idea of me going and laying down with Patty and the baby.

Standing in the doorway of my bedroom watching Patty sleep was nice. Patty is just simply beautiful. Her long auburn hair is spilling out across my pillow. Her mouth is slightly open and her lips look so soft. I would love to lean down and kiss her softly to wake her up.

Finally, I went to the side of the bed Patty is sleeping on and sat down next to her. The bed moving doesn't wake her, so I give her shoulder a gentle shake. "Patty."

She moans softly but doesn't wake.

"Patty. Come on. You need to wake up," I said and gave her shoulder a harder shake.

I saw her eyes open a little and close again. Suddenly, she sat straight up in the bed, knocking me to the ground. "Where's the baby?"

Laughing, I picked myself up off the floor. "Your mom has her."

"Oh my God!" Patti cried. "I didn't hear her wake up."

Mandy stepped into the room with Mattie on her shoulder. "That's because I came and got her as soon as she started waking up. I wanted you to get a good rest. I know you didn't get much sleep at the hospital." Mandy brought the baby to Patty. "She's been up for almost an hour now. I think she's getting tired though. When you get her back to sleep, why don't you come out and have breakfast with us."

"Okay," Patty said, taking the baby and kissing her tiny mouth. Laying back on her back, Patty put the baby on her chest and rubbed the baby's back.

I sat on the edge of the bed and stroked Mattie's soft hair. "She's so beautiful."

"Thank you," Patty said and kissed the baby's head. Patty yawned and then shook her head. "Sorry. What time is it?"

"A little after eight," I said continuing to watch her and the baby.

"How late did you guys stay up last night?"

"One," I answered. "The second movie wasn't that good and we were all dozing by the time it ended." I let my hand move to her hand that was on the baby's back. Our eyes met and I wondered if she was thinking about the moment last night when we almost kissed. I'd wanted to kiss her so badly.

"Food's getting cold," Mandy called.

"Okay," I called. "I'm going to go back to the kitchen and let you get up. Mandy and Dad are cooking bacon and eggs," I said standing.

"I'll be in there soon," Patty said looking at the baby. "She's asleep."

Turning, I left the room. When I got to the kitchen, Mandy and Dad pulled away from each other. It was obvious they had been kissing. I grinned and took my coffee cup to the pot to refill it. "Patty will be out soon."

I like Mandy and I think she's going to be good for Dad. He's been a lot happier since the two of them started hanging out. Dad had been in kind of a funk for the past year. I've often wondered if he'd been depressed because he felt like he'd wasted so much time dealing with my mother's bullshit. I'm sure he stayed for me and my brother, but it would have been okay with me if he would have ended things with the wicked witch sooner. Being forced out of the closet might not have been as painful if I hadn't had to deal with her disappointment, anger, and meanness.

Patty padded into the kitchen a few minutes later. I got a mug down from the cupboard. "Two sugars?" I asked holding up the cup.

She nodded. "How'd you know that?"

"I've watched you make your coffee a few times in the mornings before you left for school," I said as I poured the steaming liquid in the mug. When I finished doctoring the drink to her liking I sat it down on the kitchen table in front of her.

"How you want your eggs?" Mandy asked everyone in general.

Dad and I both said, "Over easy."

Patty made a face and said, "Scrambled."

I helped Dad butter the toast. "What are you doing today?" he asked me.

"Mostly planning," I said. "I'm going to get John and Jesus started on planting the new bushes at Principal Whipple's house tomorrow. The roofers are supposed to meet me at the new project first thing Tuesday morning. And I've got to go over plans on another project before I go back to Mandy's house to meet the cabinet guys."

"Wow, sounds like you have a busy week coming up," Dad said.

"Yep," I agreed.

"What about you?" he asked Mandy.

"We'll go home and do laundry, probably start painting upstairs," she said.

"And you?" he asked Patty.

"I'm going to nap on and off with my daughter," she said. "Maybe watch some TV or read. It's my first day of freedom, so I'm just going to chill mostly."

"Good for you," he said. "That precious baby is going to keep you pretty busy with feedings every few hours."

"I know," Patty agreed. "And I'm going to enjoy every minute."

Chapter Thirty-one
Patty

Listening to Mattie's soft breathing is such a soothing sound. I could lay like this and listen to her all the time. We're snuggled up in my new bed. I still can't get over how beautiful this room is. I would never imagine I'd have a room this nice again. It reminds me a lot of my room in the house we lived in with Dad before he was killed. I love the colors, they are so bright and cheery.

Today marks the beginning of a new chapter in my life. I'm no longer a high school student. I am a mother, and at some point in the relatively near future, I'll have to think about getting a job. Mom told me I didn't have to worry about doing anything except taking care of Mattie in the first six weeks of her life, but I know I'm going to get bored.

I need to get up and get some coffee. Hopefully, Mom left some for me before she headed off to work this morning.

I hate the thought of leaving Mattie alone in the bed, but she's sleeping soundly, and I know she's not going to roll off. Finally, I convince myself that she'll be okay long enough for me to get coffee and come back.

When I get back to the bedroom, she's still sleeping. I sat in the chair next to the bed and watched her some more. I'm so utterly fascinated by everything she does. I never expected watching a baby learn about the world around her would be so much fun.

As I look around the room, I'm amazed again at how quickly Richard and Theresa put this room together. I knew John and Jesus started painting the room while I was at graduation practice, but for them to move all the furniture in and set it up in the two days I was gone was pretty amazing. I suspect that Theresa and Richard brought in more help than just John and Jesus to get it done. I doubt either of them will admit it. That's okay. I appreciate what they did. Now, if we could get Mom's room ready too, that would make things even more fantastic.

With that thought, I decided that was what I was going to do today. There's a door that opens between our two rooms. I can move Mattie's bassinet close to the doorway. That way I can listen for her and work on Mom's room.

I got up and went to Mom's door and opened it. The room had been painted a light blue-green color with white trim. Mom's mattresses were sitting on the floor. The four-poster bed she had shared with my father was waiting to be put together. She told me roughly how she wanted the room to be set up. I could start putting the bed together and moving some other furniture that was sitting in the living room into her room. When she gets home tonight, we can finish organizing the room the way she wants.

Now that I had a plan for the day, I decided to get dressed and get started.

As I worked in Mom's room and took breaks to feed and play with Mattie, my thoughts went to Theresa and the way she had looked at me the night before last in her bedroom. She'd wanted to kiss me and probably would have if my mother had not walked into the room. And, I had wanted to kiss her, this time there wasn't a point to prove. I'd just wanted to feel her lips on mine.

I like Theresa, a lot, but I don't know if I'm ready to be in a relationship. It doesn't matter that she's a woman. The boys I've dated have ranged from academic geeks to football players, even some of the artsy guys I've dated have not done anything to keep me interested in them. There have been a couple of girls I might have dated if I'd have felt something for them, but that was just it. I didn't feel anything for anyone I've dated other than friendship.

I'm truly afraid of the fact that I like Theresa so much as a friend that I'm afraid my feelings won't move past that. Although, I kind of know that's not true. I have had a longing around Theresa that I can't explain. It's more than wanting to be friends or to just be with her. It's almost like I need to be near her, and it feels like it gets stronger every time I see her.

Last summer's thing with Caleb had been about the drugs. Caleb always had them, and he gave them to me because I was with him. Well, I guess I wasn't really with him. Basically, he was trading the drugs for sex, and, at that point in my life, I didn't care.

Now, what I do really matters. I don't want to hurt anyone, especially not Theresa, but how will I know that what I feel for her is more than friendship or even a passing infatuation. I guess only time will tell what will become of our relationship.

Looking down at Mattie while she is starting to nod off, I worry that something I'd done drug wise might have hurt her in those early days of my pregnancy. I stopped everything when I found out I was pregnant, which totally pissed Caleb off. Even though he was already back with Destiny, he wanted to keep me on the side as his plaything. Once I stopped the drugs, I had no use for him.

Caleb was the only guy that I'd had sex with so his denying the baby was his pissed me off. The more I think about it, the more I can't wait to get the paternity test back and shove it in his face.

This was how Theresa found me when she let herself in the house. I was sitting on the couch feeding the baby and fuming about Caleb.

"What's that face for?" she asked as she came over to the couch and sat next to me.

"Thinking about shoving the paternity test in Caleb's face when it comes back," I admitted.

Theresa chuckled. "I wouldn't dwell on that. Can I have her?" Theresa asked. "I want to hold her before I get dirty."

"Sure," I said and put the spit-up rag on her shoulder. "She's ready to burp."

Theresa nuzzled the baby's face making her smile before putting her on her shoulder and patting her back. "So how's your day been?" she asked.

"Good. I've been working in Mom's room trying to get it finished." I turned on the couch so I could look at her. "I still can't believe just you, your dad, John, and Jesus finished my room in two days."

Theresa grinned. "We might have had some help from a band of elves."

"Elves, huh?" I shook my head. "Well, I really appreciate it."

"It was your graduation and baby shower gift all in one," she said giving me that adorable grin that I find very enchanting. We looked into each other's eyes for several seconds until Mattie broke the spell with a loud burp.

"Wow, that was a good one," Theresa said and pulled Mattie up from her shoulder. "Eww."

I laughed as I took the spit-up rag and wiped Mattie's mouth. Mattie seemed to think it was funny because she smiled and cooed. "You want to get another kiss."

"No thanks." Theresa made a face as I took Mattie from her. She turned to me then and said, "Not unless you're the one doing the kissing."

I blushed and looked away. "Are you sure you want one from me?"

"Well, that depends on what it means," she said, tilting her head to search my eyes.

"You know I like you," I said meeting her questioning brown eyes.

"But," she said and raised an eyebrow.

"But, I've not done well with relationships, and after last summer with Caleb, well, I am afraid I'll hurt you," I said hesitantly.

"Why do you think you'll hurt me?" she asked.

I shrugged. "I don't know. I get bored with people. I haven't met anyone who I wanted to spend a lot of time with. I enjoy spending time with you, but I want to take things slow and make sure what I feel for you right now is not a result of hormones in overdrive. That wouldn't be fair to you."

"Thank you for being honest, and considerate. You're right. We should make sure that what you're feeling is more than just hormones because if nothing else, I'd like for us to be friends," Theresa said.

"Me too," I agreed.

She leaned in and kissed me lightly on the lips. "But, I don't think an occasional stolen kiss will hurt."

I watched as she got up and headed for the front door. "The guys will be here anytime, and we'll be putting in the last of the new trees."

"Okay," I said and watched her leave. Once she was gone, I touched my fingers to my lips. I meant what I said about taking things slow for her sake. I've always been a little flaky when it came to relationships. But no one had ever made me feel this way with a simple kiss.

Chapter Thirty-two
Theresa

I've decided I'm going to go for this thing between Patty and me. There is something there. I think there has been since I first saw her four years ago. We just didn't get a chance to know each other back then. I think she feels the same way about me. Patty says she's afraid I will get hurt. I think she's really worried that I will hurt her. That will never happen.

She may also be concerned that her having a child will be a detriment for me, but I fell in love with that baby the second I laid eyes on her. Being there to see Mattie come into this world had been so amazing and I'm looking forward to watching her grow. I've always loved kids and expected that I would adopt at some point, but now I won't have to. Patty is coming with the complete package. Now, I just need to help her understand that we are meant to be together.

As I help the guys load up our tools at the end of the day, I'm trying to come up with an excuse to come back to see Patty. I'd stay now if I weren't so nasty. A shower is going to have to happen before any snuggling.

Thunder rolled across the sky and I looked up to see the darkening clouds. I know Mandy had asked Dad to go out shopping with her tonight. She was going to look at crown molding at Lowes and Home Depot for the bedrooms upstairs.

Maybe my excuse could be that I want to stay with Patty and the baby while it's storming since Mandy will be in Paducah. That way if there's a tornado, I can help Patty, and the baby be safe. Sounds good to me. That's what I'm going with. I grin as I look at the house. This is going to be a really cool bed and breakfast when we get done.

I can't resist, I'm going to run in one more time. I'll make sure we got all our tools, and check in on Patty and the baby.

After I went around the upstairs and made sure everything was picked up and put away for the night, I skipped downstairs in search of Patty. She's not in the living room or kitchen. Her bedroom door is ajar, and I can see that she is slouched on the bed asleep with a book in her hand. I tiptoe in and look at her sleeping form up close. I want to run my fingers through her auburn tresses, but I don't want to wake her.

I look at Mattie, who is lying on her back next to Pattie. Her eyes are closed, and her tiny arms are stretched out above her head. She's wearing pink terry cloth footed pajamas with a giraffe in the front pocket area. I want to kiss them both, but Patty would probably kill me if I woke the baby. Backing away slowly, I take in the scene before me, and I don't think I've seen anything quite so beautiful. Nodding to myself as I leave the room, I know that I'm completely in love with those two beautiful angels. And, I know I want to spend the rest of my life with them.

Chapter Thirty-three
Patty

I knew Theresa had been in the room with Mattie and me even though I didn't see her. There was a musk cologne scent in the air, and I could feel her presence had been in the room. It's a little weird that I seem to be picking up a little ESP when it comes to Theresa. I'd hoped I get to see her before she left this afternoon, but I'd fallen asleep while reading. I felt Mattie starting to stir, and that woke me up. It's amazing how alert I can become the second her breathing changes or if she moves. I used to be a pretty heavy sleeper. Funny, becoming a mother changed all that.

"Patty?"

"I'm back here," I called and got out of the bed. I picked up Mattie and went to meet Mom in the kitchen.

"Were you guys taking a nap?" she asked.

"Just waking up," I said and kissed Mattie's cheek. "She needs a butt changing and a bottle."

"I'll change her while you make her bottle," Mom said and reached for Mattie. "Come on little angel. Grandma will get you all cleaned up."

I watched Mattie and Mom. Mattie smiled and cooed at her. So far she had been a very happy baby, thank God.

Mom came back into the kitchen a few minutes later with Mattie in the crook of her arm. She reached for Mattie's bottle and popped it into the baby's waiting mouth. Thunder rumbled outside. I'd heard it thundering on and off all afternoon. When I saw a flash of lightning and rain coming down hard, I turned to Mom. "Are you sure you should go to Paducah tonight? Is it supposed to rain all evening?"

"The weatherman said it was going to rain and that there was a possibility of thunderstorms, but that's not something to keep me from going to Paducah. Now if the storms are going to be bad, well then, we might have to go another time," Mom said.

I went to the back door and opened it. The wind just about jerked the door out of my hand. Looking up I could see that the sky was getting darker and off to the west there were several flashes of lightning. "Let's pull up the weather on your phone and see what they're saying now," I suggested.

"It's in my purse," Mom said, nodding in the direction of her big brown shoulder bag.

I opened her purse, and her phone was on top of everything else. Taking it out, I opened the browser and pulled up the local weather. "Oh my. There's an awful lot of red on this radar."

"What's it saying?" Mom asked patting the baby's back.

I scrolled down and found the forecast. "Heavy thunderstorms with dangerous winds and lightning," I read out loud. "Supposed to last all night." I looked up at her. "Chance of tornados."

Mom shivered. We'd had a bad run-in with a tornado when I was little, and we lived in a small three bedroom house. The tornado had gone through our yard and tore off the roof. Fortunately, that was all the damage it did, but none of us had gotten over it. Even when Dad was still alive, he would start freaking out when there was a mention of tornados. When Mom and I lived in the Section Eight apartment, we didn't worry too much. We were on the bottom floor in the middle of a concrete building. It would have to be a big tornado, and it would have to hit the building directly in the middle to get to us. Now, though, we're in this older home with a lot of windows. Granted the outside was brick and we could get in the closet in my room, and we should be okay, but it would be better if this place came with a basement. Maybe that's something we should consider having built.

Mom's phone rang, scaring the crap out of me. I almost dropped her phone. It was Richard according to the readout on the screen. I answered the call. "Hello."

"Hey," Richard said. "How are you?"

"Good," I answered.

"How's little Mattie?" he asked.

"She's good. Mom's burping her. Did you need to talk to Mom?"

"Yeah, I think we may have to cancel our road trip," he said.

"We were just discussing the same idea. I'll let you talk to her," I said and held out the phone for mom.

She handed me the baby, who had just burped loudly, and took the phone. "Hey, hon," she said.

Richard must have told her the same thing he'd said to me because she said, "Yeah, that's what we were talking about. It does look awful bad."

Mattie burped loudly again, and I took her into the living room so I could sit down and finish feeding her. Mom came in the living room a few minutes later. "Hey, Richard wants to know if we want to go out to his house. He has a basement, and the weather stations are already tracking tornadoes not too far from here."

"Sure," I said. "I'd much rather be somewhere where there's a basement if they are talking about tornadoes being close by."

Mom nodded and then said into the phone, "We'll get some things together and head out there. Do you want me to pick up some food?" She turned and went back to the kitchen.

I continued to feed Mattie and mentally made notes of what we would need to take: diapers, bottles, formula, bottled water, extra clothes.

Mom came back into the living room a few minutes later. "I'm going to start packing some things for us while you finish feeding the baby. Richard wants me to stop by Kentucky Fried Chicken and pick up a family meal for the four of us."

"Okay, she's just about done," I said as I watched Mattie sucking hard on the nipple. "We're going to a safe place, Sweetie," I said to her and kissed her nose.

By the time I'd finished feeding Mattie, Mom had almost everything we would need packed. "Be sure to get some extra clothes for you in case we have to spend the night again."

The thought of sleeping in Theresa's bed where her scent was so strong sent a rush of heat through me. But, she might not want to give up her bed two nights in a row. That would be fine. Mattie and I can sleep on the couch and Mom can sleep in Richard's room if she wants. I mean, we're all grownups, and they may not be sleeping together yet, but I'm sure they are headed in that direction. And, I'm happy for Mom. Richard seems to be a real nice guy, and they used to be in love years ago. Maybe it's going to be a good second chance for them.

I handed Mattie to Mom while I picked out some night clothes and an outfit for tomorrow. Mom gave Mattie back to me and took a load out to the car. I put Mattie in her car seat and covered it with a blanket.

The rain let up a little as I rushed out to the car with Mattie. Once she was fastened in, we took off for KFC and the outskirts of town where Richard's house was.

When we got to the house, Richard and Theresa were waiting on his front porch with umbrellas and it was a good thing. The rain was coming down hard and fast. They both ran out to the car. Theresa handed me the umbrella and then reached into the car. She grabbed two of the bags in the backseat and unbuckled Mattie's car seat. I reached in and grabbed the car seat, and we rushed together under the umbrella to the house. Mom and Richard were ahead of us. Once we were all inside the house, I lifted the blanket off Mattie's car seat. She was sleeping, thankfully.

Mom took the food to the kitchen and Theresa took our bags to her room. Richard had the local news on the television. The weatherman was talking, and they were showing the current radar. It didn't look pretty. We were getting ready to be in a tornado watch area as the worst part of the storm raced toward us.

"Come on; I'll show you where the basement is," Theresa said when she came out of her room.

I followed her into the kitchen and saw Mom and Richard standing next to the laundry room door. Mom turned and looked at us. "Richard was showing me where the door to the basement is."

"That's what Theresa was going to show me," I said.

At the far end of the laundry room was a trap door in the floor. Richard reached down and pulled the door open. I could see the narrow set of stairs leading to a very dark room below. "It's an old root cellar that I've never gotten around to finishing, so it's damp and musty, but we probably wouldn't have to be down there long if we do have to go in there."

Mom and I both nodded. We didn't care. As long as there was a place to get away from a tornado, that was all that mattered.

"Let's eat before the food gets cold," Mom suggested.

We all headed back into the kitchen. Theresa got plates down. I found the silverware, and Richard poured us all some sweet tea. We sat down at the table to eat, but Richard got up after a few minutes and went to check the weather again.

The wind was blowing very hard. It was frightening just listening to it roar outside. All of us picked at our food and watched the wind bend the trees. Finally, we stopped trying to eat, wrapped everything up and put it all in the refrigerator.

Mattie was still sleeping soundly in her car seat that I kept at my feet. I picked it up and took it into the living room and sat down at the end of the couch where I'd sat last night. Theresa came and stood next to me. She put her hand on my shoulder. "Scared?"

"Yes," I admitted. "I hate tornadoes."

"Me too," she said and sat down in the chair next to me.

"I wish I could sleep that peacefully," I said looking down at Mattie.

"I can when it's just raining, or with maybe a little thunder, but not with storms like this," Theresa said. She reached out and took my hand. "It's going to be okay though. You're safe here."

I looked into her eyes and felt like her words had a double meaning. Not only was I physically safe from the storm, but that I would be safe with her love. It was so amazing that we were both having these feelings even though we hadn't done more than have a few kisses, hugs and working side by side. Smiling, I squeezed her hand.

This thing between us seemed so sappy and silly, like something out of one of those Christian romance books I'd read in junior high. There was not inappropriate touching or sex for those couples until after marriage, but they fell in love with each other's souls. I remember thinking at the time that it sounded ridiculous, but Mom wouldn't let me read the racier romances until I got older. Even in some of those, the couples fell for each other before they became intimate, so maybe it could happen like that.

Mom and Richard came into the living room, and Theresa let go of my hand with a gentle squeeze.

A bright flash of lightning showed through the windows, followed by a loud clap of thunder that shook the house. I looked down at Mattie to see if it woke her. She put her tiny lower lip out and started to cry. I picked her up and held her close. "It's okay, baby." She wasn't going to be that easily soothed, so I stood and started pacing, bouncing her on my shoulder.

"I'll get her a bottle ready just in case the lights go out," Mom said.

"Good idea," I agreed. "Go ahead and make two."

Mattie slowly started calming down as I talked to her in soothing words.

"We should make sure our phones have good charges," Richard said. He got up from his recliner at the same time Theresa got up, and they both went about checking on the phones.

I watched the weatherman talking about places that tornadoes had been spotted. One was just twenty miles north of us. I didn't want to go into the basement until it was really necessary because it was going to be musty and I didn't think that would be good for Mattie, but I also thought we needed to prepare for going down there. "Do you guys have any blankets and flashlights we can take down into the basement?"

"There are flashlights and candles down there," Richard said, "but we'll gather blankets to put on the washer and dryer to have ready to go with us if we need to go down there."

I continued to pace, and I watched everyone preparing for us to go into the cellar. Finally, we all sat back down and watched the weatherman telling about what was going on around us.

Luckily, the storm passed through without any tornadoes close enough to warrant us going to the basement, but by the time everything had calmed down, and the tornado threat had passed I was exhausted. I fed Mattie again and then asked Theresa, "Can I sleep in your bed again?"

"Sure," Theresa said and stood.

She followed me into the bedroom and helped me get the comforter pulled back. I got Mattie settled into her sleeping position and turned to find Theresa directly behind me. "I know we're taking things slow, but I want to do this," she said as she cupped my face and kissed me.

This time it was not a quick peck, but a slow kiss. Her lips moved against mine in a soft and slow dance that had me gripping her arms and feeling my body heating up. Finally, she pulled back and looked into my eyes. "I hope that was okay."

"Yes," I said breathlessly. "Yes, it was okay."

Mom coming toward the room stopped anything else that might have happened, but Theresa had opened the door to us exploring the sensual part of this relationship. I wanted to find out where it would lead us.

Chapter Thirty-four
Theresa

Today has been the longest day. The storm last night messed up two of the yards my team was landscaping. We spent the whole day cleaning debris and trying to salvage what we could of the projects we'd started. I would have preferred to spend the day at Mandy and Patty's house finishing their yard, but the prediction of more storms coming this evening forced us to put these jobs first.

By the end of the day, I was a muddy mess and tired. I called Patty to check on her and the baby during our lunch break. She was hanging the new curtains her mother had ordered for the living room and dining rooms. I suggested that she and Mandy might need to come back to our house tonight if there were threats of tornadoes again. Patty said her mother suggested the same thing.

We both knew that Mandy had snuck into my Dad's room last night after Patty was asleep. I don't know why Mandy thought we wouldn't notice. Patty was up with the baby twice after Mandy had left my room.

I went into my room, laid down on my bed, and talked to Patty while she fed Mattie. We talked about the bed and breakfast and the baby, but we didn't talk about the growing physical attraction we are both feeling. I was okay with that because we need to be completely alone when we have that talk. Well, I guess Mattie could be there, but we wouldn't want to be somewhere that my dad or her mother might walk in on the conversation.

I'm still not sure how Mandy feels about Patty and me being together. I know that she sees it coming, but she hasn't given off any vibe about how she feels about it. I'm sure she's afraid for Patty, especially after everything Patty went through last summer.

Patty seems unsure about where our feelings are going to lead us. I'm sure she's just as afraid. Both of us have had bad experiences in the past, but Patty's the first girl I've talked to who isn't all about feminism, or partying and games. Even Linda had been into the head games a little bit. I've often wondered if she was just experimenting all along and that was why it had been so easy for her to be converted back to heterosexuality.

Watching Patty over these past few months, I've seen her mature quickly. She had seemed a little spoilt when we first started working on their house. Now, she seems more focused and determined to build a good life for herself and the baby.

When I finally called it a day for everyone, I was exhausted. We moved three truckloads of trees and branches. Tomorrow I'll split my teams up. One crew would run the wood we'd collected through the chipper, and the other team would go out with me to do more clean up and damage repair, especially if tonight's storm does more damage.

Today, Patty would be going to the courthouse with Mattie to do the paternity test. It would be four to six weeks before the results came in. I know she thinks it is pointless, but the lawyers agreed it needed to be done.

The Dalton's had money and influence, and I have to admit I'm a little afraid they will try to take the baby from Mattie, but I don't see the judge allowing that to happen. Based on Caleb's behavior, the judge should see that their family has serious problems.

I wish there were more I could do to help Patty with the Dalton issue, but there just isn't anything. After I get my shower, I'm going to go over to Patty's house and see how she's doing. Maybe Mandy won't be home so Patty and I can talk.

I'm hoping Patty is willing to take a chance on me. Every time I get near her, I just want to wrap her in my arms, hold her and kiss her. I hope that the vibes I've been getting from her mean that she wants that too.

When I got home, Dad was already there. "Hey, you're home early," I said as I entered the kitchen.

"Yeah, I had to get away from the office," he said.

"Why, what's going on?" I asked as I got a can of soda out of the refrigerator.

"Well, besides all the damage that the storm did to a couple of our new construction jobs, I had two subcontractors skip out of town after they got paid for a job they hadn't quite finished." He took a drink of the beer sitting in front of him. "I'd had a bad feeling about those guys, and I shouldn't have paid them until they were completely done. Now, I'm going to have to go out to the houses they were supposed to be finishing and take care of it myself."

"That sucks. You want me to swing by when I get done tomorrow afternoon and help you?" I sat down at the table across from him and took a drink from my soda.

"No. You need to focus on getting Mandy's place finished. She's hoping to open before Labor Day," he said.

"I know. I'm going to go over there after I get a shower and make a list of what needs to be done next. I'm sure we'll have to redo some stuff in the yard, but I'd like to get the excavating team out there to create the parking spaces on the backside of the yard." I watched Dad as I talked and he seemed to be very distracted. "Is there something going on I need to know about?"

"No," he said with a sigh. "It's just days like this that make me hate dealing with subcontractors."

"I wouldn't anymore," I said. "You're better off to use your hourly guys who you have more control over."

"I know," he said, but I still felt something was bothering him.

"Are you sure there's not something else you want to talk about?"

At first, I didn't think he was going to say anything, but then he said, "You know Mandy, and I have been getting close again."

"Yeah," I said, praying that they hadn't already broken up.

"Well, I like her a lot."

I raised an eyebrow.

"And, I'd like for us to go away together for a weekend, but I'm afraid she won't want to leave Patty and the baby alone for two days," Dad said. "I think Patty will be fine, but Mandy is worried about Caleb being out of jail and possibly being stupid enough to try to mess with Patty again."

"Caleb's out of jail?"

"Yeah, his stupid father paid the high bond," Dad said, shaking his head.

"I'll watch out for Patty," I volunteered. "I'll talk her into coming out here."

"I know, but I think Mandy's a little worried about you two being alone," he confessed.

This was exactly what I was afraid of. "Dad, we're two grown women, not children, and it's not like I'm going to get her pregnant or something like that."

Dad frowned at me. "She's just worried about Patty jumping into something because of everything she's been through."

"I'm worried about that too," I said. "But is it really that, or is she worried about Patty being with a woman?"

"I don't know," he admitted. "But, I think you need to get the job finished before anything further happens between you and Patty."

Sighing heavily, I said, " I know."

We sat there not saying anything for several minutes. Finally, I said, "I'll try to make sure the job is wrapped up in the next two weeks, barring we don't have too many more storms like these."

"Okay. I won't ask Mandy to go away for the weekend until you're done with her house," Dad said.

I nodded as I got up. "I'm going to get a shower, and I think I'll put off going over there until tomorrow. I'm too tired tonight." I turned and walked away.

He didn't move to get up. I wondered how hard that had to be for him to tell me that. Not as hard as it was going to be for me to avoid Patty for the next few weeks while I finished their project.

Chapter Thirty-five
Patty

I knew Theresa had been busy cleaning up the damage caused by the storms we'd had lately, but I could tell she also was avoiding me. We'd talked on the phone and texted each other. Our conversations had been about what we both wanted out of life, which was pretty similar. Neither of us was interested in being super rich. We just wanted to be comfortable with a beautiful home and decent income. I wanted to continue working with art. Theresa wanted to build her own construction company.

We'd talked over the phone about the kisses. Theresa admitted that she'd had a crush on me for a long time. I realized that I felt things with her I'd never felt with anyone. Still, she had intentionally avoided being alone with me for over a week. Her contract on the work at the house was almost complete, and I was worried I wouldn't get to see her when the work was done.

She was supposed to be at the house this afternoon going over everything and making sure there weren't any problems that needed to be fixed. Mom was going to be at work, and I plan to corner Theresa and get some answers about why she's been avoiding me.

I cleaned and played with the baby while I waited for Theresa to come by. Mattie was staying awake a little longer each day and had just fallen asleep for her afternoon nap when I heard Theresa's truck pull into the new drive at the side of the house.

There was a knock at the door, and I answered it. Theresa was standing on the porch looking up at the porch rafters. "There's a wasp's nest up there," she said pointing to the paper wasp nest farther down the porch.

I stepped out onto the porch and looked up to see a few of the nasty little beasts flying around the nest. I hate wasps, bees, and anything else that stings. "I will call the exterminator and have them get rid of it."

She nodded and looked back at me. "How've you been?"

"Good," I said. "Do you have time to visit for a little while?"

Smiling she said, "I suppose I could spare a few minutes for you."

I took her hand and pulled her into the house behind me. After I shut the door, I turned to face her. "I want to know why you have been avoiding me."

"What?" she asked, trying to look surprised.

"Don't play innocent with me," I said. "We've talked on the phone, but you've managed to avoid being alone with me for over a week. Have you changed your mind about seeing where these feelings between us lead?"

"No, not at all," Theresa assured me and took my hands in hers. "Can I be completely honest with you?"

"Of course," I said as I looked up into those beautiful dark eyes.

"I wanted to finish the job before we started being anything more than friends, just in case your mom is not happy about it," Theresa explained.

I raised an eyebrow. "Why wouldn't my mom be happy about it?" I asked, even though I knew there was a possibility that Mom might not be comfortable with my being in a romantic relationship with Theresa.

"Really?" she asked. "Do I need to spell out all the reasons she might not be happy about your being with a woman?"

Shaking my head, I said, "No, and I do understand why you were avoiding me now that you've pointed out the problem with Mom." I stepped closer so that our bodies were touching. "But she's not here right now."

"I realize that," Theresa said quietly, letting go of my hands and sliding her arms around my waist.

She was probably five inches taller than me, so I had to lean up to meet her lips with mine. This kiss was intense from the start. I'd missed her and had been thinking about kissing her every day. Apparently, Theresa had been thinking about kissing me too.

My hands moved up Theresa's back trying to pull her closer. This was the most passionate and deepest kiss we'd shared. If I'd had any doubts about whether I was attracted to her, they were banished by this kiss. I could actually feel my toes curling from the power of it.

Finally, Theresa moved her lips to my ear and asked, "Where's the baby?"

"She's sleeping," I whispered and moved my lips to her neck. Her skin was soft and warm. I would have easily let her take me to my bedroom and make love to me, but Theresa slowly untangled herself from me.

"As much as I would like to take that kiss to the next level, I promised myself we would take it slow. I want you to be sure that being with me is what you really want," Theresa said.

Taking her hand and squeezing, I looked into her eyes. "I know, but kisses like that make it hard."

She blushed and ducked her head. "That was another reason I was avoiding you," she admitted. "I was afraid I wouldn't be able to keep my hands off you."

I smiled and blushed too. "I'm afraid that might be a problem for both of us." I let go of her hand and moved back a step or two. "How about we plan on going out on a date after you finish the contract with my mom?"

"That sounds great," Theresa said. She looked at her watch. "I'm going to go upstairs and check my punch out list. I'll come by your room before I leave."

"Okay," I said. "I need to check on Mattie anyway. I'll see you in a bit then."

Nodding, she turned and started up the stairs. I watched her disappear before going to my bedroom to check on Mattie, who was still fast asleep in her bassinet.

I'd already spent the bulk of the morning cleaning the house. The more furniture Mom added, the more dusting that had to be done.

We were planning to visit some other bed and breakfasts so we could get some ideas about entertaining our guests. We knew that most guests would just be interested in having a place to sleep and an excellent breakfast, where others would expect to be entertained.

I busied myself straightening Mattie's clothes and diapers while I waited for Theresa to come downstairs. It felt like it was forever before she finally knocked on my open door. "It looks like we're done, but your mom has to give the final approval. Can I peak in on the little angel?"

"You have to give her mother a kiss first," I said moving closer to her.

"I think that can be arranged," Theresa said, putting her hands on my hips and pulling me to her. This time the kiss was gentle but thorough. When Theresa pulled back, she said. "I'm glad we're done. I hated avoiding you. I missed seeing you and the baby."

"We missed you too," I said and wrapped my arms around her neck.

Theresa put her arms around my waist, and we just stood there holding each other. This was something I never had with anyone else. There had only been a little hugging with the boys I'd dated, but that was really more of them groping me. Caleb never hugged me. Anytime he touched me it was sexual. Just being held like this was nice. Finally, Theresa planted a light kiss on my lips and let me go. She walked over to Mattie's bassinette and reached for the baby. "Look who's awake, Momma." Theresa nuzzled Mattie's neck and gave her a bunch of little kisses. "Aunty Theresa would love to stay and play with you, Sweetie, but I have to go back to work." She handed Mattie to me and said, "And I think she's stinky, Mommy."

"Gee, thanks." I laughed.

Theresa held her nose and backed out of the room. "I'll talk to you later."

"She's so silly," I said to Mattie and kissed her lips before laying her on the bed and getting ready to change her diaper. "But, I think Mommy is falling in love with her. That's a little scary." Mattie's answer was to coo. I think she might be in love with Theresa too.

Chapter Thirty-six
Theresa

Holy Cow! That first kiss almost melted the metal in my steel toe boots. It was the first time I had initiated a kiss with Patty, and I had not been able to contain the strength of my love and attraction. It was all I could do to keep my hands in the appropriate place. Now that I've allowed myself to believe that Patty might be falling in love with me, I've been having all kinds of fantasies about making love with her. I keep reminding myself that it's only been a few weeks since she had the baby, so she is probably not ready to make love, but that doesn't stop me from thinking about it.

Now that I've completed the project for Mandy. I plan to talk to her about how I feel about Patty. I want to reassure her that I will never hurt Patty, and I'll take things as slow as I can so Patty can be sure that this is what she really wants. But, too many more kisses like that and I'm not sure how slow we will be going.

I finished going back around to both of the other jobs I'm running for Dad and checking on the crews before I went home. Focusing on what I was supposed to be doing was really hard because I couldn't stop thinking about that kiss. I could still taste the sweetness of her mouth and feel her tongue moving across mine.

When I got home, Dad was in the kitchen cooking dinner. I went to the refrigerator and took a beer out.

Dad turned to look at me. "Rough day?"

I sat down at the kitchen table. "I need to talk to Mandy about Patty and me."

The sound of grease splattering was all I heard for a few moments, and then Dad asked," Has it become serious?"

"Yes," I answered and took a drink of the beer.

Dad didn't say anything for several minutes. Finally, he asked, "Are you sure about this?"

I looked at him. "Why wouldn't I be?"

Sighing, Dad turned from the stove and looked me directly in the eyes. "Patty has been through a lot in the past year, and I have no doubt you would not play games with her, but I want you to be sure about your commitment to this relationship before you make it."

I sat there stunned for a few minutes. Was my father accusing me of playing games? "I wouldn't want to talk to her mother if I wasn't serious," I snapped.

"I didn't mean that the way it sounded," Dad said. "Mandy is just worried about Patty."

"Don't you think I know that?" I said. "I know what Patty has been through. She and I have talked, and I wouldn't do that to her." I took a deep drink of my beer.

Dad turned off the stove and took the hamburgers off that he was cooking. "I know that," he said and came to me and put his hand on my shoulder. "I know you would not do anything to hurt Patty, and we'll just have to convince Mandy of that."

We didn't discuss Patty and me after that, and I was glad. I wasn't sure what I was going to do if Mandy didn't approve of my relationship with Patty. Being with Patty has become so important to me that I'm entirely focused on us having a future together.

The next morning I decided I was going to talk to Mandy as soon as she got off work. I sent her a text message asking her to meet me at her house that afternoon.

I was a nervous wreck the rest of the day. In fact, I was so distracted that John asked me if I was sick. There were a few times I felt like I might be sick when I thought about what Mandy's reaction might be.

By the time I finally left the job to get cleaned up and head to Mandy and Patty's house, I was a complete nutcase.

Patty answered the door when I knocked at precisely three-thirty. That was the time that Mandy and I had agreed to meet. "Hey, beautiful," she said and pulled me to her for a kiss. This one was not as soul-searing as the one we'd shared the other day, but real close.

"You're the one who is beautiful," I said after I could breathe again.

"You're so sweet," she said and kissed me lightly on the lips.

Looking around the room nervously, I expected Mandy to pop into the room anytime. "Where's your mom?"

"She's not home yet. Why?" Patty asked as she took me by the hand and led me to the couch where Mattie was sleeping.

"We had planned to meet this afternoon," I said, sitting at the end of the couch away from the baby so I wouldn't wake her.

"To talk about the house?" Patty asked as she straddled my lap.

I looked up into those amazing green eyes. It was hard to focus on anything but the heat between my legs and her lips with her on my lap like this. "I was meeting her to talk about you, or us, rather."

Patty grinned. "Were you going to ask my mother's permission to date me?"

I blushed. "Yes."

"That is so sweet," she said and kissed me again.

This kiss started out simple but quickly grew into almost a full making out session. That's how Mandy found us when she walked into the living room and said, "What the hell!"

Patty jumped back and almost fell off my lap. I grabbed her before that happened. We both quickly stood and stepped away from each other.

I was at a total loss for words and stood there shuffling my feet while Mandy glared at both of us. Finally, Patty said, "Mom, there's something we want to tell you."

"No shit!" Mandy growled.

"That's why I wanted to meet you this afternoon," I said, still not looking her in the eye. "I wanted to tell you that I'm in love with Patty."

Patty came to me then and put her arm around my waist. "And I'm in love with Theresa."

Mandy shook her head, went to the couch and looked down at the sleeping baby. Patty and I watched as she stared at Mattie and then turned to look at us. With a heavy sigh, Mandy sat down on the couch next to Mattie and gently stroked the baby's soft hair. "I suspected something was going on with the two of you, but I'm not sure how I feel about it." She looked directly at me. "Not that I think there is anything wrong with being gay, I am just worried that Patty is jumping into this without thinking about what it means in the long run."

"And what does it mean in the long run, Mother?" Patty snapped. "That I won't have a man to take care of my daughter and me, or that I won't go to college, which I didn't plan to do anyway, or that I'll be ridiculed for being a lesbian. Maybe it's because I will have to explain to people why my daughter has two mothers and no father. Yes, I made some huge mistakes last year, but trust me, this is not a mistake, and it's not something I just jumped into." Patty looked up at me. "It's something that I've thought about very carefully. In fact, I've always wondered why I seemed to gravitate toward the queer kids at school until I started understanding my feelings for Theresa. I was never really into guys the way Daria was, but I thought it was just because all the guys at our school were jerks, except for the gay guys. Now, I understand that I just hadn't met the girl who made my heart beat fast every time she came around until I got to know Theresa."

Mandy looked down at Mattie and stroked her head some more before looking back up at us. "Well, I know there's nothing I could do even if I didn't approve. You're both adults. And, I can't say I'm surprised. I'd seen the changes in both of you. I just don't want to see either of you get hurt."

I looked at Patty and grinned. "You run that risk every time you open your heart to someone. Only time will tell, but I think we're going to be fine."

Patty put both arms around my waist and hugged me, and I hugged her back. Mandy smiled and got up to join our hug. "Well, at least I won't have to worry about her ending up with another asshole like Caleb."

"That is true," I agreed, relieved that things went better than I thought they would.

Chapter Thirty-seven
Patty

It's hard to believe that a little over a year ago I started on a journey of self-destruction and today I'm healthier and happier than I've ever been. It's a beautiful mid-summer day. Mattie is in her bouncy chair playing with her mobile while I'm planting flowers in the flower beds in the yard. My gorgeous girlfriend, Theresa will be here later this evening and we'll have the whole house to ourselves because my mom is going to spend the night with Theresa's dad.

Mattie is still sleeping a lot, so we'll have plenty of time alone while Mattie naps. Theresa and I have had some major making out sessions, but tonight will be the first time we're going to make love. Theresa insisted we would wait until after my six week checkup so the doctor could make sure my body was ready for sex.

It is really sweet that she wanted to wait and make sure everything was okay with me, but it's been driving me insane. I want to do so many things to her and have her do them to me. Tonight, we're both going to get to know each other's body's very well.

After few hours working in the gardens, I decided to take a break and go inside. Mattie was napping in her chair, so I thought this might be a good time to paint for a little while. I was rounding the corner of the house when I saw the mailman stop in our drive. He got out of the mail truck and walked toward me. "Are you Patricia McNeal?"

"Yep," I said.

"I've got a certified letter I need you to sign for," he said holding out an envelope with a green postcard like thing on it.

I put Mattie's bouncy chair on the ground, took the letter and signed where he pointed. It was a letter from a lab, which struck me as weird that I would have to sign for it. He handed me a few other pieces of mail and then got back in his truck.

Shrugging, I put the mail in the bouncy chair next to Mattie, picked up the chair with her in it and went into the house. After I washed the dirt off my hands, I changed Mattie's diaper and put her in her bassinet. I put the bills in Mom's bill basket and picked up the letter opener sitting next to the basket. With a quick flick of the blade of the opener, I'd sliced the envelope open from the lab. I pulled the letter out and read it. I had to read it twice for the full meaning of it to set in. This was the paternity test results that Caleb's father had insisted we get. The results said that Caleb was not Mattie's father. I fell into the chair next to Mom's desk. My stomach churned forcing me to the bathroom where I threw up until there was nothing left but dry heaves.

I sat on the floor of the bathroom and thought about all those times last summer that I woke up and didn't remember where I had been or what I had done. Apparently, during one of those blackouts, I'd had sex with someone, or someone had taken advantage of me, and Mattie was the result. I wanted to be sick again, but there was nothing left to throw up. Mattie's cries were the only thing that finally got me up off the floor.

I went into our room with tears continuing to flow down my face. I picked Mattie up and kissed her cheek. She looked so much like me, and it was hard to see anyone else in her face. I would probably never know who her father is. There had been a lot of guys at the parties. It could have been any one of them.

I took Mattie to the living room after I changed her diaper and fed her while sitting on the couch. I sat staring into space while Mattie slept next to me on the couch. This was how Mom found me later that afternoon.

"I figured you'd be getting ready for your big night," she said, putting her purse down on the chair by the door.

When she looked at me again, I burst into tears. Mom rushed over to me and wrapped me in her arms. "What happened? Did you and Theresa have a fight?"

Sobbing, I shook my head and buried my face further into her shoulder. After a few minutes, I started to calm down, and Mattie started to cry. I guess my crying woke her. Mom reached over me and picked the baby up. "Hello little angel," Mom cooed at the baby and kissed her forehead. She put Mattie on her shoulder and then looked at me. "What's going on?"

"I got the paternity test results today." At mom's questioning look, I said, "Caleb is not the father."

"Oh," she said with a whoosh of air. "Wow."

"Yeah," I said and started crying again. "And I have no idea who the father is."

Mom leaned over with the baby, and we did a group hug for several minutes. Finally, she sat back and bounced Mattie on her shoulder. "You know what? That's okay. Unless you need to know who the father is, I say we don't worry about it."

I shrugged. "Not really. I mean, I had no intention of letting Caleb have much of a role in Mattie's life, if any, after the way he was about everything." Sighing, I said, "It just really upsets me that someone took advantage of me, and Caleb let them." I looked at her. "I didn't tell you about some of the rumors going around about me. Some people said that Caleb was pimping me out, and that I'd participated in an orgy. I refused to believe it when I heard it, but now it makes me wonder."

"Sadly, Caleb didn't get everything he deserved for what he did to you, but what goes around comes around," Mom said.

"Not for people like the Daltons, Mom. Anyway, you're right, it doesn't matter who the father is. Since it's not Caleb, we won't have to worry about the Daltons messing with Mattie or me," I said, but then a new wave of sadness hit me when I realized I would have to tell Theresa about this. What was she going to think? She might even change her mind about being with me when she finds out what a slut I was.

Mom noticed the change in my expression. "What now?"

"I'm going to have to tell Theresa."

Mom squeezed my hand. "She'll understand."

"I hope so," I said and then Mattie decided she was done waiting for us to finish our conversation. She was ready to eat, and she was ready now.

Chapter Thirty-eight
Theresa

I knew something was wrong when I saw that Mandy's car was still parked behind the house. She was supposed to be meeting Dad at five, and it was four forty-five. I parked my truck next to Mandy's car. Apprehension set in as I approached the back door. Mandy was in the kitchen talking on her cell phone. Based on the conversation, I could tell that she was telling my dad that she was running late. She gave me a wary look, which added to my fears.

Patty was sitting in the living room on the couch with Mattie in her arms. Mattie was sucking on the nipple of her bottle, and her tiny hand was wrapped around Patty's thumb. It was the most beautiful sight. Every time I see them like this I am overwhelmed by the feeling of love I have for these two lovely angels.

When Patty turned to look at me, I could tell she'd been crying. I immediately moved to sit next to her and put my arm around her shoulder and pulled her into my embrace. "Hey, what's the matter?"

She looked into my eyes with such sadness, and I was terrified she's going to say she can't be with me. But, she leaned toward me and kissed me lightly on the lips before saying, "I got some interesting news today."

"Yeah?" I asked and kissed her temple.

"Yeah." She looked down at Mattie who was starting to nod off. "I got the paternity test back."

I'm surprised that getting the paternity test back has her this upset. She was pretty sure she knew what the result was going to be, and then it hits me. "Caleb is not Mattie's father."

Patty nodded and started crying. Mandy came into the room and took the baby. "I'll put her to bed."

I'm dumbfounded. Patty was so sure that Caleb was the father. She said she hadn't slept with anyone else. But, she'd also said that there were a few times she'd blacked out and didn't remember how she'd gotten home. What Caleb not being the father said about what had happened when Patty was completely out of it made me furious. I wanted to hunt Caleb Dalton down and beat the shit out of him.

Patty is crying hard. I turned her so that I can put both arms around her and hold her against my chest. "Shhh," I whispered. "It's going to be okay." I held Patty and let her cry her fill. I could see Mandy in my peripheral vision and was surprised that she was still there. Patty's full on cry had smoldered down to hiccups. I was whispering to her that it was going to be okay and wondering why Mandy is standing just inside the kitchen. Then, it hits me. Patty and Mandy are afraid I'm going to dump Patty when I figure out that she had sex with someone else. That she may have had sex with several other people and has no idea who they all are.

"Hey," I said and lifted Patty's chin trying to get her to look at me. She kept her eyes diverted. "Patty, look at me." Finally, she brought her tear-filled eyes up to meet mine. I took my thumbs and wiped at the tears as I cupped her face. "It doesn't matter who the father is. It's not going to change how I feel about you, or Mattie. I love you both, and that's not going to change, no matter what."

"But, I don't know…" she trailed off and lowered her eyes.

"Look at me," I said firmly, and Patty raised her eyes up to mine again. "I don't care about anything that happened in the past. The most important thing is that you and Mattie are healthy and happy."

"But, what if I got something from whoever it was, something the doctor didn't test for?" Patty asked as new tears start to form.

"We'll get the tests run to make sure, but that isn't going to chase me away, Patty. I love being with you. I love talking to you and listening to you. No matter what those tests reveal, I'm going to be here with you. Okay?" I studied her eyes as they turn from fearful to filled with love. I kissed her then, knowing that Mandy was still in the kitchen. With this kiss, I wanted to show Patty how deep my love for her is. I wanted Mandy to see how much Patty means to me.

When we finally pulled apart several minutes later, Patty put her arms around my shoulders and buried her face in my neck. "I was so afraid I'd lose you."

Holding her tightly to me, I said, "You aren't going to lose me."

"Do you still want to spend the night?" she asked quietly.

I chuckled. "Do you have any plastic wrap?"

Patty pulled back and looked at me. "Plastic wrap?"

"Protection, just until we do have those tests run," I said. "I don't have any dental dams."

She blushed bright red all the way to her roots. "I'm sure we do."

"Let's go look," I said and pulled her up with me. Hopefully, Mandy missed that part of our conversation, I thought as we went into the, thankfully, empty kitchen.

Chapter Thirty-nine
Patty

Theresa is sleeping soundly as I get up to fix Mattie a bottle. When I came back to the room, I turned the rocking chair, so that it's facing the bed so I can watch Theresa sleep while I feed Mattie.

Last night was amazing. I'd been a little afraid of not knowing what to do but found that my natural instincts told me exactly where to touch, where to kiss. It was indeed the first time that I had made love with someone. What Theresa and I have together will never be just sex. I can tell that every time we are intimate, it will be filled with the most profound love. Theresa made sure that I felt that. God, she is so amazing.

I was terrified that she would run when she found out that Caleb wasn't Mattie's father. I was afraid she'd think that I'd lied to her about not having been with anyone but Caleb. That had not been the case at all because she had listened to what I'd told her about the parties and that I'd often woke up somewhere and not known how I'd gotten there. She was angry that Caleb had not protected me.

Tomorrow, we are going to call my doctor and ask her to run more sexually transmitted disease tests and pray that I didn't get something I can't get rid of. I could almost start crying again when I think about how stupid I was. Looking down at Mattie's perfect little face, I know that I've been fortunate and blessed.

Theresa stirred and rolled onto her back. I stared at her perfect breasts and felt desire retake hold of me. Being with Theresa is definitely right. I'd never known how much a body could ache from wanting to touch every inch of someone.

When Mattie finished eating and went back to sleep, I slipped my nightshirt off and climbed back into bed and snuggled my naked body up to Theresa's. She only stirred a little. I looked down at her nipple and remembered how many times I found it with my mouth earlier. My mouth watered now with the need to taste her again, so I indulged myself, leaned down, and took the nipple in my mouth.

Theresa moaned softly as I stroked the other breast with my hand. My need to touch her was overwhelming. Moving my hand across her abdomen, I remind myself that we are being careful and I'll need to get protection before I go too much further. When I looked up at Theresa's face, her eyes are just slits as she looked down at me, but I can see the desire in her eyes.

Rolling over on top of her, I moved my lips across her chest to her neck, along her jaw bone to her mouth. The kiss I give her is deep and with intent. I want to make her come again. I want to hear her scream my name again.

Theresa returns my kiss with equal vigor and then flips us over, so she is on top. "I think it's my turn."

"But, I started it this time," I said.

"Wrestle you for the top," she said.

"You're on," I said and moved my hands to her ticklish spot along her ribs.

Epilogue
Theresa

Mattie is sitting in her walker and squealing as she rips the paper off her very first Christmas present. Patty is helping Mattie with the wrapping while I video the scene on my phone. The toy is a stuffed pink elephant like the one that Mattie's playdate friend has. Mattie was in love with this toy and cried after it every time she played with her little friend. Now she's holding it by its trunk, shaking it, jumping up and down, and squealing. It's a beautiful sight.

Patty looked over at me and pushed several strands of her lush auburn hair away from her face. I forget about filming Mattie as I stare into Patty's eyes. Those deep green eyes pull me in every time. I could look into her eyes forever.

Smiling, Patty swats at me. "Pay attention to our daughter."

"Yes ma'am," I said and laugh at the fake mean look she gives me.

It still warms my heart through and through when I look at these two beautiful ladies who make my life whole. Seven months ago I would never have thought that I would have a family, but here we are.

My phone rings, messing up my filming. It's Dad. "Merry Christmas," I said when I answered the phone.

"Merry Christmas," he said. "What time are you bringing my granddaughter over?"

"So you don't care if Patty and I come, you just want the baby?"

Dad laughed. "I guess you two can come too."

"Well, I guess so since Mattie doesn't know how to drive yet," I laugh with him. "What time we going to see the parental units?" I asked Patty.

Patty looked at the clock that read eight in the morning and asked. "Is Mom making breakfast?"

"I'll make breakfast if you'll bring the baby now," Dad said, hearing Patty's question.

"I don't know about that," I said. "The last time you made breakfast you burned the biscuits."

Mandy took the phone from Dad and said, "I'm making biscuits and gravy, and it should be ready by the time you get here if you leave now."

Patty started laughing. "Oh for crying out loud. We'll head over there in a few minutes."

I ended the call and started videoing Mattie opening her next gift, which is a set of keys for her to chew on because she's teething. She's not as interested in it as she is the elephant. "I think we should have given her the elephant last," I told Patty.

"Yeah, she doesn't care about anything else," she said.

"How about we give her the rest of her gifts later," I suggested. "I'm starving, and I want to get some of the biscuits and gravy your mom is making before my dad eats it all."

Patty stood and held out her hand to me. I took her hand, and she pulled me up and into her arms. "I bet we can get Mom and Richard to watch Mattie for a few hours and then we can come back here and have some fun."

"Is that right?" I asked.

"Yes," Patty said and handed me a letter.

"What's this?" I asked as I opened the envelope.

"Read it."

It took me a few minutes to figure out what the letter is telling me and then I grinned at Patty. "No more plastic wrap?"

"No more plastic wrap," she said and then kissed me.

This was great news. All of Patty's tests had come back negative. She'd been lucky, and we both knew it. But, regardless of what happened to Patty during the blackouts when she was using drugs, she didn't get any diseases, but we did get a beautiful daughter. Even now that Mattie is almost eight months old, and she's changed so much, she still looks just like Patty. We will probably never know who Mattie's father is. He was just one of the jerks that Caleb knew and whom Caleb had allowed to take advantage of Patty.

None of that matters now. We've moved past all of that and are focused on our future. Dad moved to the bed and breakfast with Mandy. Patty and Mattie moved into Dad and my house. She helps her mom with the bed and breakfast. Dad and I have more business than ever. Everyone is healthy and happy. Life doesn't get better.

But, it did a few weeks ago, when we found out that Caleb Dalton got busted for selling drugs at the University of Kentucky. He'd gotten away with using Patty and assaulting her. But, his father was not going to be able to get Caleb out of this mess. It's funny how things happen the way they are supposed to.

Patty handed Mattie's car seat to me when I got my coat on. "So what do you think about letting Grandma and Grandpa have the baby for a few hours?"

I put my free arm around her and kiss her hard. "I think it will be more than a few hours. Let's go get some nourishment so we'll have the energy for our afternoon activities."

Patty leaned back and looked me in the eye. "I'm so glad your dad talked you into taking my mom's job. Not only did you help her put together an amazing bed and breakfast, you put me together when I didn't think I'd ever find all the pieces of me again. Thank you for being my rock where I've built a mountain of love."

I kissed her again. "Thank you for letting me love you."

The End

Printed in Great Britain
by Amazon